INITIATE OF THE JACKAL

The Apprentice Of Anubis

Book 2

LAURA GREENWOOD

Visit Laura Greenwood's website at:

www.authorlauragreenwood.co.uk

Cover by Ryn Katerin Art

Initiate of The Jackal is a work of fiction. Names, characters, places, and incidents are the products of the author's imagination or are used fictitiously. Any resemblance to actual persons, living or dead, businesses, companies, events, or locales is entirely coincidental.

If you find an error, you can report it via my website. Please note that my books are written in British English: https://www.authorlauragreenwood.co.uk/p/report-error.html

To keep up to date with new releases, sales, and other updates, you can join my mailing list via my website or The Paranormal Council Reader Group on Facebook.

A Brief Note

The Egyptian Empire World is set in an alternative universe where the Egyptian Empire never fell and replaced the Roman Empire. The split in the timeline happened after the Ptolemaic dynasty and the final Cleopatra's infamous reign. Instead of Egypt falling into the hands of the Romans, they fought back and gained control of the budding Roman Empire. All religions still exist in the world, but many have been absorbed into the Egyptian religion (this was common practice during their ancient history, so is something I adopted into the series).

For the purposes of this series, the Egyptian Empire spans much of Africa and Europe, as well as some of the Middle East.

I made the decision to keep a lot of the words

and systems we use today (including place names like London and the River Thames) to make the reading experience as smooth as possible. If this was the real progression of events, those things would likely have been named differently.

Things I have kept are the Ancient Egyptian concept of a week (10 days, including a 2 day "weekend"), month (3 weeks), season (4 months) and year (3 seasons plus 5 feast days). The currency they're using is debens (derived from the Ancient Egyptian word for bread - something workers were often paid in). Names have also been influenced by Ancient Egyptian history.

Blurb

With her first mummification test looming, and her lessons about being Blessed by Anubis taking up her time, the last thing on Ani's mind is uncovering more temple secrets.

But when Nik discovers a missing body, she knows it's only a matter of time before her friend starts getting her into trouble again.

And that's without dealing with the fact she's accidentally dating Prince Ramesses.

If only the dead were the only thing she had to worry about.

-

Initiate Of The Jackal is book two of The Apprentice Of Anubis modern fantasy series with a romantic (m/f) sub-plot. It follows a new priestess in the Temple of Anubis, Ani, and her jackal familiar. It is set in an alternative world where the Ancient

Egyptian Empire never fell, and set in alternate London.

TEMPLE OF ANUBIS
(LONDON)

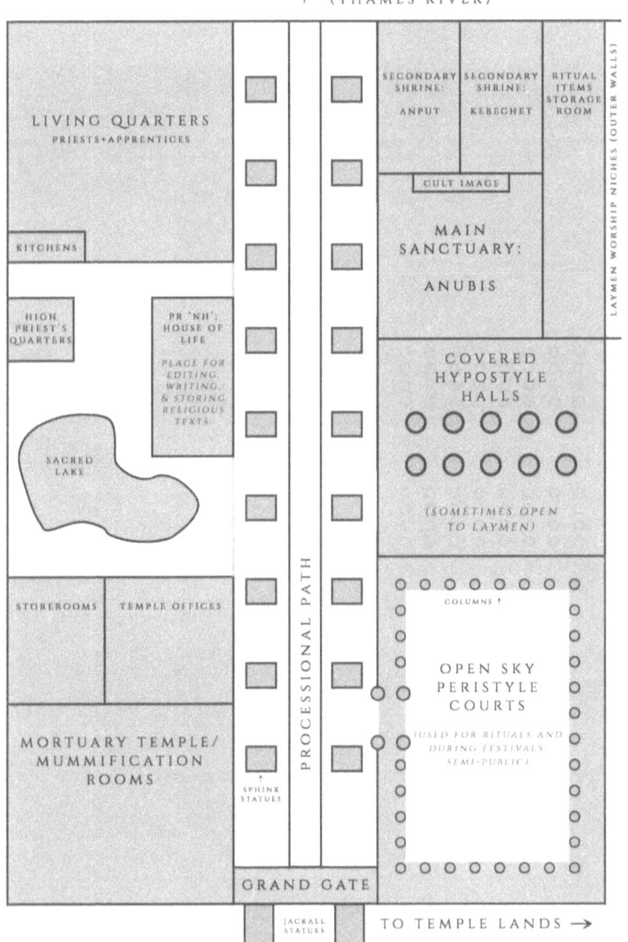

What Happened Before

Apprentice Of The Dead

Eighteen-year-old Ani attends the Day of Choosing along with the others her age living in London. While there, she is shown to be Blessed by Anubis when a sacred jackal (Matia) stops in front of her. She leaves the temple and is reunited with her best friend (Neffie) who has been assigned to serve Bastet.

On her first day at the temple of Anubis, Ani finds the High Priest's son (Nik) frustrating to be around, but as time goes on, the two develop a mutual respect verging on friendship.

When Nik asks for Ani's opinion on a mysterious tub of organs and some strange incisions on the bodies they've been working with, they find themselves investigating stolen body parts and accidentally disturb two of the thieves in the process. They manage (mostly accidentally) to catch the thieves, but are sentenced to clean up duty as a consequence of their recklessness.

Nik is about to ask Ani to spend some time with him on their rest day when Ani is asked to attend a banquet by Ramesses, the prince of the Egyptian Empire who is visiting for the funeral of the vizier of the British Isles.

Chapter 1

I never thought I'd be sad about not getting assigned to mortuary cleaning duty, but now the list of assignments is posted and I'm staring at my name, there's no mistaking how I feel.

Maybe I've just gotten used to all the cleaning thanks to mine and Nik's punishment. It's nothing to do with the fact I won't get to spend my day with him.

Not that they're allowing me back onto body preparation duty. Instead, it's like my punishment is being continued by assigning me to the front office.

My gaze slips down the list until I spot Nik's name and a brief sense of relief goes through me. It seems like he's been assigned to the front office after all. I'd still prefer to be in the mortuary, but at least I know I'll have good company while doing paperwork.

I head over, already longing for the familiar sterile scent of the mortuary at the beginning of the day. Before the chemicals start flowing through the bodies of the deceased, and we start removing organs.

I step through the front door to be greeted by a man with a bland expression.

"You must be Ani," he says.

"I am." Though it's not like I need to confirm it. I'm the only priestess in the entire temple, in training and not.

"Are you ready to start your first day in the front office?" he checks.

I force a smile onto my face. "As I'll ever be."

"This is easy, one of the best jobs."

I eye up the older man, trying to get a measure of him. Is talking to grieving relatives and logging dead bodies really his favourite part of being a priest for Anubis? I'm not sure why, but I feel a little sad for him, especially as so much of our craft is focused on the way we prepare the bodies for burial.

The door opens and Nik steps inside. "Sorry I'm late."

"Don't let it happen again," Kaaper says as he goes off into the next room, leaving the two of us alone.

Nik grimaces.

"Your father?" I ask quietly.

He nods. "You'd think he *wants* his temple to run inefficiently."

"He's probably just busy."

"I know. He's always been too busy for me, I don't really blame him, I'm not the most important thing going on in his life."

My heart aches for him. While he can have his infuriating moments, seeing past them to what made him this way makes it hard to hold that against him.

"Ready for a day filling in forms?"

He groans. "I thought our punishment was done."

I let out a small laugh, it's like he's reading my mind. "Sadly, I think this is just one of our duties now."

Nik groans. "What have I done to deserve this?"

"Maybe it's punishment for being super arrogant at the start of training."

He grimaces. "Have I ever said I'm sorry for that?"

"Not in as many words."

"Then I'm sorry."

"It's fine," I assure him. "I know you have a lot to live up to. It can't be easy."

He takes a deep breath. "So, what are we up to today?"

"I think it depends how many people come in." I gesture to the front door which heads out onto the street. It's one of the only entrances the public can use to get into the temple, especially without an invitation.

"I don't know whether I'm hoping for a busy day or a quiet one," Nik mutters.

I smother a laugh. "We have to learn all of this stuff," I remind him. "Even if it's so we know to ask not to be placed here permanently."

"I hate it when you're right."

"Is that because you have to admit that you're wrong?" I can't help the satisfied smile that spreads over my face.

"Maybe."

"Have you two not started work yet?" Kaaper demands as he swaggers back into the room.

I ball my hand up into a fist. I hate it when I'm faced with someone who assumes everyone knows what they're doing all the time.

"This is our first time in the office." Nik keeps his voice far more level than I would have done. I'm not sure how he manages it. Probably because of the amount of time he's spent dealing with his father. I imagine that can't be an easy thing to navigate.

"Right." He turns away and picks up a huge stack of parchment before marching it over to a simple desk and dropping it down. "Sort those out."

I roll my eyes and walk away before he can give us any other instructions.

I exchange a glance with Nik, but don't say anything. Technically, Kaaper is our boss until the end of the day, I'm not about to say anything that will annoy him.

The two of us seat ourselves behind the desk, both keeping a wary eye on our supervisor.

"What are we supposed to do?" I ask, hoping he knows something I don't. There's a good chance of that. He grew up here, Nik will know answers to questions I haven't even thought to ask yet.

He picks up the first sheet of parchment and scans it.

"It's a death certificate." He passes it to me.

I take it from him and make quick work of

reading it. I'm not surprised to discover he's right. For one, he has no reason to lie about it.

"What do we do with it?" I ask.

"That depends on what's on that stack." He points past me.

Now my annoyance about Kaaper not giving us any guidance has worn off a bit, I'm a little intrigued about what we're supposed to be doing.

I grab the top one and compare it to the death certificate. They're for different people, but it only takes me a moment to see what we're supposed to be doing.

"I think we need to match the death certificates to the final wishes and insurance documents," I say.

Nik nods. "I guess that makes sense."

"We should get started, the stack doesn't seem to be getting any smaller."

As soon as I say it, Kaaper comes over and drops another pile of papers on our desk. This is going to be a long day.

"Is it wrong to hope that there are some inter-esting deaths among these?" Nik asks.

I smother a snort. "We're not supposed to joke about that kind of thing."

"Says who? I think Anubis would like it."

I shake my head, mostly to cover my amusement. Personally, I think he's right. No god who deals with the dead as much as Anubis does can do so without a sense of humour. But I doubt our superiors will think the same.

Especially when we're somewhere like this and there's a chance that the general public could overhear us. I can imagine the front pages of all the news outlets saying that we're making light of death.

We soon fall into an easy rhythm of matching up the papers and labelling them with the same code that's on the body. It turns out it isn't the most interesting of jobs, but at least I get to do it with someone who makes it easier and not harder. I'm still not completely sure how it happened, but somewhere between meeting and accidentally catching someone stealing organs, the two of us have become friends. I can't say I'm too sad about it.

"Do you think we'll be allowed to deal with the bodies again soon?" Nik whispers.

"It depends if your father thinks we're done being punished."

"He never mentions it."

"So that could be that we're going to be punished for the rest of our lives, or that we're already forgiven," I mutter.

A wry smile twists on his lips. "You'd think."

"I mean, we did help stop something bad," I point out.

"And somehow, I think that makes it worse, not better. Father won't like that two of his most junior apprentices managed that when he had no clue about it."

"No matter who we are."

"I suspect the fact I'm his son, and you're the Blessed only makes it worse and not better."

I sigh. "I know this is all I ever wanted, but sometimes I think doing what Mum wanted would be easier."

"What did she want you to do?" he asks.

"She wanted me to serve Isis."

Nik lets out a surprisingly loud laugh. "I'm sorry, I don't mean to laugh."

I let out a small chuckle. "It's fine. It wouldn't have suited me. I'd probably have ended up as one of the dropouts if I'd actually started an apprentice-ship there."

"I disagree," he responds. "I've seen first-hand how tenacious and determined you are. You'd be the High Priestess within a week."

"We both know that's not even possible."

"And I still wouldn't put it past you."

Warmth surges through me at his compliment. When I first arrived, I thought that all I wanted was to prove I was a good fit to be a priestess of Anubis. Now, I realise it's only part of it. I enjoy the camaraderie of the apprentices more than I thought, and I've had a lot fewer issues over the fact I'm the only girl than I thought.

They'll probably make themselves known once I'm further up the chain of command.

But as Dad always says, there's no need borrowing trouble from tomorrow. I should focus on what's right in front of me.

Chapter 2

It's a relief to be back in the mortuary, and not just because it signals that I'm not going to be punished forever. But that doesn't stop how tired I am after attending yet another feast with Ramesses last night. He always springs them on me at the last minute, and no matter how many times I try to leave early, it never seems to happen.

I wish I felt like I could say no. But somehow, insulting the son of the Pharaoh by telling him I don't want to attend official events with him doesn't seem like the idea. Even if I do want my sleep.

I line up with the other apprentices in front of Hori. It's unusual for him to be standing here waiting for us when we come in. Now we've been at the temple for a while, he normally just posts our assignments on a board near the entrance. I'm surprised he doesn't send an email around about it. I suspect that would probably be a little too efficient for the temple.

"Good morning," Hori says, more brightly than is right for this time. "Before you get started for the day, I just wanted to let you know that your first mummification test is taking place in a couple of days. You'll be expected to complete everything from the modern mummification itself, to the wrapping and presenting of the bodies. You'll be assessed at each step of the way with points being awarded for the accuracy and neatness of the procedure, and the correct way of presenting the body afterwards."

My eyes widen. I can't believe they're testing us so soon. And right after Nik and I have spent so much time away from the bodies. It's hard enough to think through everything that needs doing when I've just done it.

"Use the next couple of days to practise and ask any questions you have. But please remember that these bodies belong to people and should be treated with the utmost respect and dignity."

I have no idea who he's aiming his comments at,

I've never known any of the people in this room to not do that. But maybe things have gone badly when there's a test on the line before. I've known some competitive people in the past, I can see how it could become a problem.

"All right, no reason to dally. Get to work everyone," he dismisses.

I head over to the table assigned to me, relieved to find there's a body under the sheet. It's good to be back working on actual embalming. This is far better work than the front office or cleaning up the mess everyone creates while preparing the dead.

I lose myself in my work, dimly aware of the others in the room doing the same thing. It isn't just the apprentices who started with me either, but more senior priests too. It means that if we run into any problems, we have people we can ask.

Around the room, small machines full of chemicals whir. None of the bodies in this room are being traditionally mummified, that's done in a different preparation room. Perhaps it's one we'll get to see once we've completed the first test.

I stifle a yawn, trying to focus on the body in front of me instead of how tired I am. I'm positive I'm not making any mistakes, but it's taking everything I have to keep on track.

"Have a good date last night?"

I turn around to find a smug-looking Nik grinning at me from the next table over.

"It was a nice night."

"But a late one?" He waggles his eyebrows suggestively.

My eyes widen. Is he really trying to insinuate *that*? "Yes, but not like you're thinking."

He needs to get those ideas out of his head and keep quiet about them in front of other people. The last thing I want is for rumours of what my relationship with Ramesses is like getting around. Especially when they're not true.

"So how long is it until we're going to have to call you Princess Ani?" He's trying to sound light still, but there's something off in the way he's talking, but I have no idea what could be causing it. No doubt he'll tell me about it when the time is right.

"Are you jealous, Nik? Do you want to be the girl on Ramesses' arm?" I ask as sweetly as I can manage, not wanting to delve into anything deeper while we're busy mummifying.

Surprise flashes over his features. "Why wouldn't I want to be? You make it sound so fun." He's trying to be funny, but it comes out bitter.

"I think you'd make a great couple." A small

part of me wants to wink at him, but the rest is still trying to make sense of the way he's acting.

"And people would celebrate me throughout the empire."

"Careful, your imaginary ego might be getting the better of you," I tease.

Nik chuckles. "Don't worry, that will never happen."

"I'll believe it when I see it."

Nik's machine beeps, signalling that it's done pumping embalming fluid around the body on his bench. He waves at it, effectively telling me that he needs to get back to work.

Which is fair. I do too.

I'm aching by the time the day ends. It's hard work, but I always feel a sense of accomplishment knowing that I've managed to prepare someone for their journey into the afterlife.

"Have you got plans on going to the Tamesas festival?" Nik asks as we make our way back to our rooms.

"Mmhmm. I wouldn't miss it. I go every year. You?"

"Of course. Father's always given the priests and apprentices half a day off to go if it isn't already their day off."

"That's nice of him. I know a lot of High Priests wouldn't do that for a festival dedicated to another god."

Nik lets out a small laugh. "You're not wrong there, but he believes it's important that we celebrate Tamesas, just like they celebrate the Nile in Egypt."

"I agree." The Thames is such an important part of the life of the city, it makes sense that we celebrate the god who embodies it.

"Are you going with Ramesses?" he asks.

I shake my head. "He hasn't asked. Which is good."

"Good?"

Is it me, or is there hope in his voice?

"I've always gone to the Tamesas festival with Neffie, I don't want that to change." Especially for someone who seems more interested in who I am than me.

Maybe I'm judging Ramesses too harshly. We've been on several dates, but I don't feel like I know him very well. It's probably partly on me too. He never gives me much warning before picking me up, which means I never really have time to rest before seeing him.

"That sounds nice."

"It will be," I agree. "I don't see Neffie nearly enough." It's a definite drawback to the two of us training at different temples. I try to message her regularly, but somehow days and weeks slip by without me noticing.

We enter the building. The other apprentices head right in the direction

"Are you heading into dinner now?" he asks.

I shake my head. "I need to take Matia out. She's been cooped up in my room all day." I hate that she has to spend all her time in my room and not by my side. I wish there was something I could do. I did try sending her to the keepers who work with the rest of the sacred jackals here at the temple, but Matia had only ended up more stressed, and I didn't like that at all.

"Want company on the walk?" he asks.

I flash him a grateful smile. "Thanks, but I'll be fine. It's nice to just clear my head after a day in the morgue."

He nods. "That makes sense."

"Maybe tomorrow? I just want to process everything, especially when this is the first day we've been allowed to work with the bodies again."

"I hear that. I'm glad our punishment finally seems to be over."

"Don't say that, it'll end up undoing it and we'll be back on clean-up duty by the end of the week."

"Only if we get into more trouble," Nik points out.

"Sometimes, I think trouble is unavoidable when you're around."

"I promise I'll try not to get you in any more."

I raise an eyebrow. "Why don't I believe you?"

"On Anubis' life, I won't get you into more trouble."

"See, you're only moments into your promise and you're already leading me into blasphemy." My amusement shines through my voice, but that's okay. I want him to know I'm only messing with him.

"A jackal can't change his nature."

"More blasphemy?"

He chuckles. "If you want blasphemy, I can tell you all the things the priests used to say when they didn't think I was listening as a kid."

"I'm sure you're not supposed to be compromising my mind. I'm Blessed, remember."

"And does that stop you from remembering all of the bad things you've ever heard?"

"Obviously."

"Then I take it as my personal mission to re-corrupt your mind."

I let out a small snort. "You can try. But it'll have to wait for later. I need to sort out Matia."

He nods. "See you in a bit. Give her a scratch for me."

"I will do." I wave and head towards the stairs, a smile spread over my face.

Chapter 3

Perhaps I should be thanking Ramesses for keeping me up late the day before yesterday. Being so tired meant that I passed out last night instead of ending up unable to sleep while I worry about what's going to happen today.

From the tired expressions on several of the others' faces, they haven't fared as well and are showing signs of fatigue.

I wish I could make it better for them. I'm not foolish enough to think this is a competition. We'll all pass and fail on our own merits, and I want everyone to pass otherwise we're going to end up short-handed at the end of our training.

Metal tables line up neatly in the secondary mortuary room, each with a body covered in a sheet. I stand behind the one labelled with my name and wait for the go-ahead to start body preparation.

Hori enters the room and stands at the front, clearing his throat to call our attention to him. Not that he needs it. Everyone's eyes are glued on him.

"You may begin," he says.

There's a flutter of activity around me, but I pay it no attention. Instead of pulling the sheet straight off, I pick up the chart of my deceased. Unlike when we first arrived, the woman's name is written on the top along with the log number. While the latter is the most important in terms of tracking bodies through the temple and making sure they're delivered to the right family and tomb, the former is important for the preparation of everything else.

Do I need to put in the order for the coffin and other funerary items? I know I need to deal with the amulets and charms that will live in the wrappings, but I don't know about the rest of it.

Thankfully, the test lasts several days. That's plenty of time to find out what needs doing.

I push those thoughts aside. I'll worry about those things after I've dealt with the initial embalming.

I scan the clipboard so I know what to expect.

Thankfully, there's nothing particularly surprising on the sheet. The woman died of natural causes and doesn't have anything about any surgery on any of her major organs. That's going to make my life easier, which makes a lot of sense. This is only the first mummification test, they don't want to trip us up just yet.

Satisfied I've learned everything I need to, I set the clipboard down and start preparing my equipment, leaving the woman covered in the sheet.

I don't pay any attention to any of the other apprentices, they're doing much the same thing that I am, it's not particularly interesting.

There aren't normally this many embalmings going on in this small space, and it's starting to make itself known from the harsh smell of chemicals filling the room. I'm not sure if it's my imagination, but there's a sting in my eyes.

I push past it and focus on setting everything up so I can drain the woman's body of blood so I can replace it with embalming fluid. The whole process is almost second nature to me, and it's only when I'm mostly done that I realise most people would probably find it a nausea-inducing job, but I'm well past that. Preserving the dead for their journey to the afterlife is an honour I'm happy to undertake.

There's none of the normal chatter that goes along with our embalming. It's interesting, as Hori never explicitly told us we couldn't talk to one another, but somehow we've all fallen into silence.

I switch on the machine that will pump embalming fluid through the body and check over each of the connections to make sure it's running properly. The fluid should push out the remaining blood and do its part to preserve the tissue within.

Once I'm satisfied everything is set up correctly, I pull out the clipboard again so I can start making a note about which amulets I need to collect from the store. I doubt I'll need to have any of them custom-made this time as they'll be trying to give us all the same set-up, otherwise, it wouldn't be fair.

I take a moment to check how everyone else is doing. Nik seems to be doing the same as I am, which isn't surprising, while several of the others are just setting off the embalming fluid machine.

Next to me, Ibi is looking a little bit less confident. He's holding a scalpel a little higher than necessary.

"Ibi," I whisper, checking that Hori isn't paying any attention to us. I don't think helping is off-limits, but I want to be sure.

"Huh?"

"You're going to cut a bit high." I point to my own incision.

Ibi's eyes widen. "Thanks, Ani."

"Any time." I flash him a quick smile before turning my attention back to the task I should be focusing on, confident we haven't drawn any unwanted attention with our exchange. Hopefully, it'll be enough to make sure Ibi gets back on track, though I'll keep an eye on him. So long as I don't let my attention slip too far from my own assignment, I don't think it'll be too much of a problem.

The next few hours slip by surprisingly quickly. The only interruption being Djou asking if anyone had a spare trocar after his broke.

Hori didn't say anything about that, so I have to assume there's nothing against asking one another for assistance. I imagine we'll all get a chance to talk about it once we're all at dinner. I might need to make Matia wait a little longer for her evening walk to make sure I have enough time to talk to every-one. If I fail the mummification test, then it could be the end for me as a priestess, and I don't want that.

Then again, will they fail me? Being Blessed hasn't made much difference to me yet, but failing me would probably make all of us look bad.

Though that's not a particularly comforting thought. I don't want to pass just because of who I am.

I'm just going to have to make sure there's no risk of that.

Chapter 4

I double-check the message from Hori telling me that I'm excused from the mortuary today so I can meet with my Blessed mentor. It's hard to believe it's finally the day I get to meet him and start learning about why Anubis picked me. Not that I'm complaining.

"Come on, Matia," I call to my jackal, pleased that I get to spend an extra day with her.

She trots up to me, her tongue hanging slightly out of her mouth. I reach down and ruffle the fur on the top of her head and she lets out a satisfied rumble in response.

"We're going to go find out more about ourselves," I tell her. "It's going to be a lot of fun."

Nerves flutter within my stomach as I make my

way out of the accommodation building and towards the covered hypostyle hall. I shouldn't be surprised that's where the Blessed mentor wants to meet me. It's away from anywhere the public will visit uninvited, but also won't be too busy this far away from any of the holy days.

The cool air brushes against my skin, and I wish I'd thought to bring a jumper with me. With all the moving around and lifting I have to do in the mortuary, it's easy to keep warm despite the room being kept at a corpse friendly temperature at all times.

"Good morning."

I spin around to find a thin man wrapped in a thick wool coat standing in front of me, with a large jackal standing by his side.

"Morning," I manage to squeak.

"You must be Ani," he says.

I nod, at a loss for what else to say now I'm faced with the person who knows more about me than I do about myself.

"I'm Khafre, I've been assigned to teach you the ways of the Blessed," he responds, his accent barely discernible but definitely there.

"It's nice to meet you." My nerves come through my voice.

"Don't worry, I've done this before. I've trained all of the Blessed from your generation."

"I didn't think there were many," I mumble.

"Not in the British Isles, no. But around the world there are several, though not as many as there have been in the past, we're in a little bit of a Blessed Apprentice drought. But you're the newest and the most unusual."

A blush rises to my cheeks and I hate it. Why should I feel self-conscious about the fact I'm the only living Blessed priestess serving Anubis? It's the god's choice who he bestows his favour on, it's not like I asked for it.

"Why don't we have a seat?" He gestures to a pair of mats.

Is it a suggestion, or an order? It's hard to tell. I'm not sure where Khafre sits in the order of command here at the temple.

But I don't want to make him dislike me when he's the one who can unlock whatever abilities I have.

I make my way over and seat myself, patting the ground for Matia to come lie next to me.

To my relief, she behaves and does as I've asked.

"I see you're doing well with your jackal," Khafre observes. "I don't think I've seen a Blessed getting on with their jackal so early in their relationship."

"Matia has made it really easy," I respond.

Khafre nods. "I wasn't so lucky. Beni here was a nightmare to begin with." He ruffles his jackal's ears. "She's mellowed with time."

"Does that mean I have to worry about Matia getting more unruly?"

"Probably not, especially once you connect with her more. Part of the Blessed magic allows us to create a type of communication with our jackals."

"I'll be able to talk to her?"

He lets out a small laugh but shakes his head. "I'm sorry, no. But you'll be connected in a way that means you'll be able to understand her in a different way. It's hard to explain unless you've experienced it yourself."

"I see."

"It's one of the easiest parts of our gift to learn, so it's normally what we start with. We'll move on to the more complicated aspects in future lessons," Khafre continues.

"How long are you going to be here for?" I ask.

"It depends how long you need me. Typically, I spend six months to a year with a Blessed student, but it has been known to last longer."

"Oh."

"That's why I was late coming to meet you. My last student took a little bit of extra time." Something about the way he says it makes me think that there might be more to it, but I don't ask. "Often I find that the apprentices who take the longest are the ones who don't believe they're worthy of Anubis."

"How do you know I do?"

"That's a good question," he acknowledges. "It's something I can tell. I've also been given your transcripts from Hori, I know how you're performing in the mortuary and how your superiors view you. I heard that you managed to stop an organ thief a month or so ago."

I blush furiously. "It wasn't single-handed or anything."

"But you still took your role as an apprentice seriously enough to do it."

"I don't think the High Priest felt like I was taking anything seriously."

Khafre's lips quirk up into a small smile. "He's just doing his job."

"I know. I just wish he wasn't so hard on Nik."

"Do you mean Nikare? I've heard rumours about him being difficult."

Anger raises its head within me. "He isn't."

Khafre holds up his hands in defence. "It's okay, I didn't mean anything by it. I've never met him, I'm sure he'll prove the rumours wrong when I do."

I nod, trying to contain my annoyance that there are rumours like that about my friend. Mostly because I can see where they can have come from. Nik doesn't make the best first impression.

"Is this helping to gain control over my bond with Matia?" I ask.

He smiles serenely. "Would you believe me if I said yes?"

"You're here to teach me, so I'd believe you."

He raises an eyebrow. "Most people answer no to that question. But you're right. I've found the process goes a lot smoother if I have a good sense of my student. It helps build the trust in what I teach."

"That makes sense."

"So, want to tell me more about Nikare?"

I shrug. "There's not much to tell. Nik has a lot of expectations on him and I think it shows in the way he interacts with people when he first meets them. Once you get past that, he's intelligent, thoughtful, and determined. I'm lucky to have a friend like him."

"I can tell you have a good deal of respect for him."

"I do."

"And how are you finding life at the temple?"

"It's different from what I expected, but I think that would be true of serving any of the gods," I answer honestly.

Khafre laughs. "I think you might be right about that."

"Did you always know you were going to serve Anubis?" I ask him.

Surprise flits across his face. I'm not sure if it's because I've asked him a question, or because of what it is. I don't suppose it matters.

"Actually, no, I didn't. I thought I was going to enter Thoth's temple. It's what my parents wanted for me, and my teachers. But that's not how things worked out."

"Do you regret not serving Thoth?" Will I be feeling regret in a few decades' time?

"No, never. If I hadn't joined Anubis' temple, I wouldn't have had the bond I share with Beni, and I wouldn't have found the purpose I have."

Relief floods through me. I reach out to scratch Matia's head, already feeling closer to her, even if the bond hasn't solidified yet.

"What do we do next?" I ask.

"I need you to place your hand on Matia's head, much like you're doing already. You need to keep contact with her, but it doesn't matter what or how, you just need to keep touching her."

"That's easily done," I admit. I tickle her behind the ears.

"And then you need to focus on your connection to Anubis."

I frown. "How do I do that?"

"We can try silent meditation."

I grimace. "Somehow, I don't think that's going to be the best way."

Khafre chuckles. "Perhaps not. But luckily for you, there are other ways. Because you've already been here a while, we should be able to use the method where you talk about your time here. It should be enough to focus you in the right way."

"Okay. Where do you want to begin?"

"Maybe we should start with how you felt about Anubis before you came here."

I take a deep breath. I've never really admitted any of this to anyone before, though Neffie does know some of it. "I always felt a pull towards this temple whenever I passed it, and I wanted to serve Anubis, but knew it wasn't likely."

"And then everything changed?"

I nod. "I went to the Day of Choosing and when it came time for the sacred animals to come out, Matia appeared. I didn't realise she was going to stop in front of me until after she'd already done it."

Khafre chuckles. "I felt the same with Beni. My friend had to poke me to get me to respond appropriately."

"It was so surreal."

"And then you came here for your first week?" he prompts.

"Yes."

"How did it make you feel to be in the mortuary for the first time?"

"A little strange," I admit. "Especially with all the new people around. I was really worried about how people would treat me and if they'd act differently because I'm female."

"Have they?"

"Not really. Though I still find it weird when people double-check who I am. Shouldn't it be obvious?"

"Perhaps. But I imagine they're being polite."

"That's what I tend to think." It certainly seems that way most of the time. "But no, I didn't feel like anyone treated me any differently. I like it that way, it makes me feel like most people believe I can serve just as well as the rest of them."

"Mmhmm. And how do you feel when you're preparing a body?" Khafre asks.

"I don't think I can really explain it. But there's something peaceful about it."

He continues to prompt me with questions about the process of mummification and how it makes me feel connected to Anubis and the worship in the temple. I'm not sure how any of it is going to help me feel connected to Matia, but I'm willing to trust him.

"All right, I think that's enough for today," Khafre announces after a while. "How do you feel?"

My first instinct is to say that nothing has changed, but I stop myself before I do. There *is* something different, even if I can't put my finger on it. "I don't know," I admit.

Khafre nods. "That's okay, it'll probably take a while for things to change. But you should watch how you feel when you talk to Matia over the next few days."

My jackal responds to her name by pushing her head against my side.

I give her an extra scratch.

"I'll see you again soon," Khafre says. "But I'll be around the temple still, so if you have any questions, just drop me a message and I'll get back to you."

"Thanks." It feels strange to have someone here because of me. No one else is going to have one-on-one sessions with a senior priest like this.

For the first time since the Day of Choosing, I actually start feeling like I'm special, even if I have no idea what that actually means.

Chapter 5

I smooth down my formal dress and pace up and down the hall, trying not to draw more attention to myself than necessary.

"Everything is going to be fine, Ani," Nik says from his seat on the bench.

"Have you ever given evidence in the Hall of Ma'at before?" I ask.

"No."

"Then you don't *know* that it's going to be okay."

"Of course I do, we didn't do anything wrong," he points out. "We stopped Minnefer and Bebi from stealing organs. All that's going to happen is that we'll go in there, tell them what happened, and then they'll dismiss us," he points out.

"I suppose."

"And it's not like we lied at any point either. We've only ever told the truth."

"Which means Ma'at's priestesses won't be able to catch us in a lie. I know that, but I'm still worried."

Nik gestures to the seat to his side.

I give a deep sigh and sit down next to him, resisting the urge to fidget uncontrollably.

"I never thought you'd be the nervous type," he observes.

"Do you not remember the fridge?" I mutter.

"Believe it or not, I do remember that, yes. What I remember was someone brave. And a luckily placed jackal."

I smother a snort. "Are you saying that it was Matia who actually saved the day and stopped the organ thieves?"

"That is kind of what happened."

I let out a laugh and I shake my head. "If only they could interview her instead of me."

"That would be handy," he agrees. "But I promise it'll all be fine."

"You'd better be right," I mutter.

A priestess steps into the hallway and heads towards us. "We're ready for you now," she says. "Which of you would like to go first?"

I exchange a glance with Nik.

"You should go, you'll feel better once you're done," he says.

"Thank you." I get to my feet and nod to the priestess. "I'm first."

"Follow me," she responds stiffly.

"Good luck," Nik calls after me.

Oddly, I do feel a bit better now he's talked to me.

The priestess leads me into the next room. A huge scale sits in the middle of it, with a single chair on one side, and a panel of priestesses on the other.

"Sit," the priestess with me instructs, pointing to a lone chair.

I take a seat and fold my hands in my lap.

"You should be aware that the scales will report any falsehoods you tell," the priestess says.

I nod, my nerves returning even though I don't want them to. It's like Nik says, if I tell them the truth, it's not going to be a problem.

At least Minnefer and Bebi aren't in the room. I half expected them to be, which shows how little I know about the justice system.

I should probably pay more attention. While the priests of Anubis aren't responsible for investigating any suspicious deaths, but with the number of dead bodies we deal in, it's inevitable that we find proof of foul play sometimes. If that's the case, then I suspect the people who find it will end up in the same chair I'm sitting in now.

"State your name and occupation."

"Ankhesenamun, Blessed Apprentice from the London Temple of Anubis." My voice shakes, but I'm not sure whether or not they can hear it.

The scales in front of me don't move, which I assume is a good thing.

The priestess checks her list of questions. "How do you know Nikare, apprentice from the London temple of Anubis?"

"We started our training at the same time," I say. "And we're friends." I'm not sure whether they need to know that, but you can't catch organ thieves with someone and not call them your friend.

"What about the accused?" she asks.

"Bebi was one of the priests training us in embalming. I only knew Minnefer in passing." My heart is pounding, but I think being able to see the unresponsive scales in front of me is helping with my nerves a little.

"In your own words, tell us what happened," the priestess says.

I take a deep breath and tell them everything I

remember about the strange situation that led to being stuck in a freezer and accidentally incapacitating Minnefer and Bebi. Saying it out loud makes me realise just how justified Nik's father was in punishing us for being reckless. Especially considering we abandoned our posts in order to pursue it.

I won't be so foolish next time.

A scribe writes down everything I'm saying, but no one seems to be responding much to it. They've likely already heard this dozens of times while interviewing the people involved. Bebi himself didn't seem to be a particularly strong character, he'd probably broken during their questioning in the end. I know I would just from sitting in front of them for ten minutes.

"Thank you, Ankhesenamun, you may go now," the priestess says once I've finished talking.

I get to my feet, hesitating as I reach the door. Should I thank them for their time?

A quick glance back reveals the priestesses are already talking among themselves, presumably about my testimony. I'm going to assume they're not expecting anything from me.

I make my way back to the main hall and wait for Nik. I assume he's talking to a different set of priestesses. If I'd known, I'd have wished him luck before I left.

A door opens and he reappears, his face lighting up into a smile when he sees me.

"Are you done?" he asks.

"I think so."

"Do you want to go grab something to eat?"

"Aren't we supposed to head straight back to the temple?" I ask.

Nik shrugs. "We could, but what are we going to do there? This is our only task for the day."

"True. I was going to spend some time with Matia, though."

"Why not both? We can go via the temple and collect her?"

My heart warms at the care he's showing towards my jackal. "That sounds good."

"Let's do that."

"Lead the way." He gestures to the exit. "I'll be glad to see the back of this place."

I raise an eyebrow. "Does it make you feel like you've done something wrong?"

"Definitely. Ma'at's priestesses are scary. I felt like one of them was going to arrest me if I looked at them wrong."

I smother a laugh. "You do have a talent for drawing the wrong kind of attention," I tease.

"Which is as good a reason as any for us to get out of here before I manage to drag you down with me."

"Again."

"If I remember correctly, you didn't take much convincing."

"And that's why it'll be impossible for you to get me into trouble again. I like to learn from my mistakes," I respond.

Nik lets out a light laugh. "Somehow, I doubt that's going to prove true."

I cross my arms and narrow my eyes at him. "And for that comment, you're the one paying for lunch."

He snorts. "Fine. Lunch is on me."

We head out of the Hall of Ma'at and back towards our own temple. I'm relieved to have my testimony done, especially as it means I get the rest of the day off. Between my work in the mortuary, my lessons with Khafre, and attending events with Ramesses, I don't feel like I've had a single moment of peace in the past few weeks. It'll be good to have an afternoon without any of that to worry about.

Even if I am spending it with Nik.

Chapter 6

I glance back at the mortuary, hoping I've done everything right with the final stage of my first mummification test. From what Hori said, they'll be examining the final wrappings and amulets tomorrow, though I'm not sure how they're going to do that without disrupting the body inside. I suppose that's not really my problem. I know Hori well enough to be sure that our supervisor won't do anything to disrespect the dead. And everyone else takes their jobs too seriously to do it too.

Well, except for the organ thieves. I suppose they didn't really care about the state they were leaving the bodies in. But that's over now.

Hopefully.

Hannu lets out a small shriek, bringing everyone to a standstill.

"It'll be fine," Ibi assures him with a reassuring hand on his arm.

"What's happened?" I ask.

"I think I missed an Eye of Horus amulet," he says, his voice shaking. "I used an Eye of Ra one instead."

"They might not even notice that," Djou responds.

"That's the kind of thing they're sure to pay attention to," Hannu counters. "And they're going to fail me for it."

"They aren't," Ibi says. "It's one mistake. So long as you haven't made lots of others, I'm sure it'll be fine."

"It's easy for you to say that, you're not the one who made it." Hannu's face is getting redder by the second, no matter how much the others are trying to reassure him.

"Can you fix it?" I ask.

"How? The mortuary is closed. I'm not going to be able to even get close enough to fix it."

"Sneak back in," Djou suggests.

"I can't do that. If I get caught, I'll be thrown out of the temple for it."

"But I won't be," Nik blurts. "I can do it."

My eyebrows shoot up. This is not the Nik I met at the beginning of training.

"Do what?" Djou asks on behalf of a stunned Hannu.

"I'll sneak into the mortuary tonight and I'll replace the amulet with the right one," Nik says.

"Are you sure?" Hannu's hopeful question almost breaks my heart.

Nik nods. "It's fine. I won't get into too much trouble, even if I'm caught."

"You can say that again," Djou mutters. "Look at how lightly you and Ani got off with your last punishment."

"To be fair, they were being punished for helping the temple," Ibi counters.

Djou shrugs. "It's the truth."

"Which is why you should let me do it," Nik says.

"Thanks." Relief crashes over Hannu's face. "Is there anything you need me to do?"

"No, I've got it all sorted," Nik promises.

"We should go get some food," Ibi says, gesturing to the doors that will take them through to the dining room.

The others all mumble their assent and they

make their way through, leaving me and Nik alone in the foyer.

I need to go and get Matia so she can have a stretch before I have something to eat. I'm not sure what Nik's doing, but he's not particularly friendly with the others. I don't think he'd ever admit it, but he's kind of a loner. I should be honoured that he even wants to be friends with me.

"That was a nice thing to offer," I say to Nik. "Are you really going to swap out Hannu's wrong amulet?"

"Of course."

"Then I'm going with you."

He snorts. "I thought you weren't going to let me get you into trouble again?"

"You're much less likely to get into trouble if I'm there with you," I point out. "I can be your lookout."

"Thanks, Ani, I appreciate it." His relieved expression is genuine.

"You wanted to ask me to help anyway, didn't you?"

A small smile lifts the corners of his lips. "How could you tell?"

"Let's call it a woman's intuition."

"Or you just know me."

I let out a small laugh. "That's more accurate," I admit.

Footsteps draw our conversation to a close. If someone overhears us, we'll never get away with the switch and Hannu could end up failing. I don't want that, and apparently, Nik doesn't either.

"Ankhesenamun," a man I don't recognise says.

"That's me. How can I help?" I don't think I have a lesson with Khafre this evening, and even if I did, he'd send me a message rather than a person to summon me.

"His Highness, Prince Ramesses requests your presence at a banquet honouring Horus tonight," he says.

I repress a groan. These banquets are normally planned weeks in advance, if not months, does he have to send me invites on the day itself? How does he know I don't have plans?

"He requests that you wear this." He holds out a box.

Reluctantly, I take it. I've been through this with several of these situations before. There isn't any refusing, either of the gifts or the invitations.

"He'll pick you up at dusk."

"Thank you," I say reluctantly.

The man disappears, having fulfilled his task.

"Another date with the prince?" Nik asks. "We really are going to be calling you Princess Ani."

"Eurgh."

"It's not a good thing?" Genuine concern comes through his voice.

"I don't want to be a princess," I admit. "I feel at home here."

"But you have to become a princess if you want to be with Ramesses."

Can I admit that I'm not sure if I want to be? The prince seems nice enough, but I wish I got to spend more time with him outside of official functions so I could actually get a sense of who he is. I don't want to spend the rest of my life with someone I don't know.

"What's in the box?" Nik asks when he realises I'm not going to respond to his comment.

I flip the lid and let out a slight gasp. Jewels glitter from the collar and matching armbands sitting within.

Nik whistles. "Wow."

"Yeah."

"No one will doubt his interest in you once they see you wearing those."

"Maybe they'll just think my family is wealthy in their own right," I murmur.

"Unless your family own an entire country, they wouldn't be able to afford these." He picks up one of the armbands and weighs it in his hand. "The craftsmanship is exquisite."

"Mmhmm."

"You don't seem particularly excited. I thought people loved getting jewels?"

"I suppose they do." But these seem to be steeped in expectations. I can't tell him that, though. I don't think he'll get it, even if jewellery is a good gift for both men and women.

I need to see Neffie so I can talk this through with someone who understands.

"I'm going to get something to eat and then take Matia out," I say, shutting the box once he's placed the armband back inside. "If we're going to go and replace Hannu's amulet, we need to do it before Ramesses comes to pick me up."

Nik nods. "I can do it on my own if you want..."

"No. I'm not letting you do this without a look-out, and since you've already promised Hannu you will, that means we need to do it in the next couple of hours. We'll eat and go."

"Thanks, Ani." He pauses, as if there's something more he wants to say. "Do you want me to keep Matia company tonight?"

"If you don't mind. I don't want her getting lonely while I'm gone."

"Consider it done. The two of us will have a great time."

I reach out and place my spare hand on his arm. "Thanks, Nik, I appreciate it." I smile at him before leaving the foyer and heading up towards my room.

Somehow, my evening has become so full that I'm exhausted just thinking about it. Maybe I should skip eating now so I can spend some time with Matia before I have to get ready. There'll be food at the banquet, so it's not like I'll be waiting until breakfast to eat something.

And if I'm only going to be keeping guard for Nik, then it won't matter if I'm already dressed for the banquet. Which means I also have time for a bath.

I'm glad I took the chance to go for lunch the other day, it seems that my personal time is disappearing quicker than I want it to.

Chapter 7

Nerves flitter within my stomach as I approach the outside of the mortuary, but I know it has nothing to do with sneaking in to fix Hannu's amulet.

I'm worried about what Nik's going to say when he sees me dressed up so formally. He hasn't exactly been hiding what I can only assume is dislike for Ramesses and what's happening between us. I'm not sure when he became so protective of me, but there's a part of me that likes it.

I check over my shoulder to make sure no one is following me and slip inside the door.

"Finally," Nik says, turning to face me. "A little overdressed for breaking into a mortuary."

I force a smile to my face. "Ramesses is picking

me up soon, I didn't think I'd have enough time to change."

"Ah, I see." He pauses. "You look amazing."

"Thank you." I glance down at the fine linen of my dress and the glittering jewels attached to the various ornamental pieces I'm wearing. I don't think I've ever worn anything quite this fancy before.

But Nik has a point, it's not exactly the best outfit for breaking into a mortuary.

Though is it breaking in if we can walk through the front door?

"I picked up a spare amulet earlier," Nik says, holding up an Eye of Horus amulet for me to see.

"You've just been carrying that around all day?"

He nods. "I figured that if anyone asked about it, I could say I had a strange dream last night and wanted protection."

"Clever."

"Aren't I?"

I chuckle softly. "Didn't I just admit that?"

"And don't think I'm going to forget it."

"I have no doubt you'll be reminding me for the rest of our lives."

He grins. "I hope so."

I shake my head in bemusement. "We should get on with this. If anyone finds us near the mummies, they're going to think we're tampering in the opposite direction."

"Hmm, good point. Come on then. You keep watch and I'll do the actual swapping."

We head deeper into the mortuary until we get to the door leading to the dry storage room where the mummies waiting to be transferred into their coffins are stored. Now they've been mummified, even by the modern method, they need to be stored in a dry place rather than in the fridge with the fresh bodies.

"Wait here, I'll be right back," Nik says.

I nod and turn to face the entrance. I fiddle with my ring, trying to decide if I'm more nervous about what we're doing, or about the banquet I'm supposed to be going to afterwards.

I think it's the latter but I can't really explain why.

"Ani?" Nik calls, his voice filled with confusion.

"Everything all right?" I call back. We should probably be a bit quieter in case someone else has decided to use the mortuary tonight. Not that it's likely. As far as I'm aware, there isn't going to be anyone on this floor after hours.

"I need you to come see this."

Despite knowing that I should stay outside and

insist we get out of here, my intrigue is piqued. I scan the room to make sure there are no signs of anyone else before slipping through the door.

The dryness makes my skin itch, but I ignore it. I won't be here for long.

"What's wrong? Are you having problems locating the amulet you need to replace?" It doesn't seem likely, Nik knows what he's doing.

"No."

Something in his voice has me worried.

"Please don't tell me we're dealing with another organ theft," I mutter.

"I wouldn't quite say that," he responds.

A frown pulls at my features. "Are you going to carry on being so cryptic, or are you going to tell me what's going on?"

"Sorry, I'm just trying to process this."

"That's not reassuring."

"It's not meant to be. Hannu's mummy doesn't have a body in it."

Shock, confusion, and horror all flood through me at the same time. "What? Are you sure?"

"Very."

"Wouldn't Hannu have noticed something like that?"

"I'd hope so, or the wrong amulet is going to be the least of his worries."

I hurry over to take a look at the mummy to try and make sense of what he's saying.

From the outside, it looks just like it should. The linen sheet that was placed over the top has been moved to the side, presumably by Nik, and the wide neat bandages beneath swaddle the form of the body closely.

"Everything looks okay," I point out.

"Touch it," Nik responds.

I glance at him, trying to work out whether or not he's being serious. I don't think he'd be trying to play a trick on me. I wouldn't put it past him on another occasion, but not when we're doing something like this.

Slowly, I reach out and press my hand against the top of the wrappings. There's something strangely squidgy about it.

"That doesn't feel right."

"No," he agrees.

"Do you think Hannu did something wrong?"

"I doubt it," Nik responds. "He missed one of the amulets because he was stressed, but I've seen him doing mummifications enough times to be sure he's done it right."

"Same. What makes you think there's no body at all?" I ask.

"This." He picks up the arm and bends it in a way that wouldn't be possible even if the embalming had gone well and truly wrong.

"Where is it?" I whisper. "And does Hannu know about it?"

"He can't," Nik says. "If he did, he wouldn't have wanted me coming anywhere near this."

"So, what do we do about it?" I ask. "We could ask Hannu?"

Nik shakes his head. "We can't stress him out more than he already is. I don't think telling him his body's missing is the best course of action."

"Fair point. What about your father?"

Nik purses his lips. "No. I don't think he'd be impressed about how we've found out."

"Then what can we do?"

"I think we just have to leave it." He doesn't look happy about that.

"But Hannu might get into trouble."

"I know. But there's nothing we can do about that."

"And what if he tells someone that you offered to change the amulet for him? Everyone heard you offer, you'll get blamed." I can't deny the panic building up within me. I don't want Hannu to get into trouble for this, but I don't want Nik to either.

"I'm going to have to risk it."

"You could get thrown out of the temple," I whisper hurriedly. "Your father can protect you from a lot of things, but I don't think he'll be able to do anything about a missing body."

"It's a chance we're going to have to take or we're all going to end up in more trouble. No one's going to like the fact that Hannu made a mistake in the first place. And the fact that we offered to help him..."

"Technically only you offered," I point out. "You're the only one who knows I'm here."

Nik snorts. "Are you going to turn on me now?"

"Of course not, you know I wouldn't do that."

"I do. But that doesn't answer what we're going to do about this." He gestures to the body lying on the table.

Well, the pile of linen. I don't think it can really be called a body at this point.

"We'll think of something," I promise.

"Maybe there's some sort of clue around about..."

"You better not be thinking about investigating

this yourself," I cut him off. "You can't get into more trouble."

He sighs. "Why do you have to talk so much sense?"

"It's a gift. And one that's going to keep you out of trouble."

"Then I will make it easy for you and promise that I won't do anything until you're back from your date with Ramesses."

I let out a small groan.

Nik raises his eyebrow. "Are you not looking forward to it?"

"I'm just tired and know it's going to be an exhausting evening of talking to people I don't know and trying to represent someone I don't know that much about."

"Do they ask you much about the temple?"

"To be honest, I'm not sure if many of them know who I am enough to do that."

"That's a shame."

"You say that, but it's probably best if I don't go around telling everyone about the ins and outs of burial preparation. It might not be the best topic for high-end banquets."

"You might be right there," he agrees. "Do you still want me to spend some time with Matia?"

"If you wouldn't mind. My room is open for you."

"Aren't you worried I'm going to go snooping?"

"Not really."

I don't miss the pleased expression that flits across his face, even if he covers it quickly.

"We should get out of here," I say. "I need to meet Ramesses."

"And here was me thinking that you wouldn't want to hang out in a mortuary after dark."

"I'm not five, I don't worry about people coming back to life at night."

"Is that something you used to worry about?" Nik asks, gesturing for me to pass through the door before him.

"Yes. I used to have a regular nightmare about it."

"Interesting. In mine, I was drowning in the Thames."

"Maybe the living dead chased you into it," I suggest.

He chuckles. "Now that would make a fun story."

"So long as I'm not the main character," I mutter.

"Oh, Ani, where's your sense of adventure?"

"You got it into trouble too many times and now it's on strike," I retort.

Nik chuckles. "That's fair."

We come to a stop outside the mortuary, each of us knowing this is where we part ways. Something strange lingers in the air between us, but I can't put my finger on what it is.

Maybe it's just because I'd rather stay at the temple and hang out with Nik and Matia rather than go to this banquet.

"Have a good time," Nik says.

"I'll try."

"I'll give Matia extra scratches for you."

I flash him a grateful smile. "Thanks for spending time with her, I appreciate it. And she does too."

"Any time, she's better company than a lot of people I've met."

I let out a small snort of amusement. "You're not wrong there." I wave goodbye and head towards the entrance to the temple, steeling myself for the banquet to come.

There's a reason I'm well suited to dealing with the dead, and it's almost certainly to do with the fact I'm not good at making small talk in a room full of people I don't know.

Chapter 8

The car pulls up in front of the temple and Ramesses steps down wearing a traditional linen outfit. His jewelled collar puts mine to shame, and his fingers are dripping with rings. He wears it all well, which makes sense considering he was born into this.

"Good evening, Ani," he says in his delightfully accented voice. He takes my hand in his and lifts it to his lips to kiss.

"Good evening, Your Highness."

"Please, call me Ramesses," he reminds me.

"I will," I promise. We have this exchange every time he picks me up, but I know enough about etiquette to know that it has to happen this way. We're not officially dating, which means that we're not supposed to be too informal all the time. It's not something I'm in any rush to change. I imagine there are a lot of things I'll have to do differently if I officially start dating a member of the royal family. It's not on my to do list.

Ramesses helps me into the car and then knocks on the front. The driver sets off, the engine whirring into gear as we travel through the London streets.

"It's still strange to be in a vehicle like this," I admit.

"Did you not have one growing up?" Ramesses asks.

I shake my head. "My family don't live far from here, we've never seen much need for one." Between the regular buses, and the fact everything is within walking distance, there's never been a use for one. Most people feel the same if the empty streets are anything to go by.

"It makes things much easier to get around," Ramesses muses. "I couldn't imagine having to walk everywhere. Or having to have a palanquin carry me around. I don't know how my ancestors managed. Have you ever sat on one?"

I shake my head.

"My mother prefers them. She insists on using a palanquin rather than a car every time there's a parade. But it's such an uneven way to travel. I don't recommend it."

"I'll keep that in mind if I'm ever given the choice."

"You should." He picks up a bottle of wine and takes a sip before handing it to me.

"No, thank you."

"You should drink."

"I have a test tomorrow," I half-lie. Technically, it's only the results that get revealed, but it's enough for me to know I want to be at my sharpest.

Ramesses shrugs. "Suit yourself." He takes another sip.

"What's the banquet for?" I ask. He never told me about the invitation, which is pretty normal. I'm not sure why he never thinks it's necessary to tell me these things, potentially because it doesn't actually matter.

"They've opened a new wing of the National History Museum and they're holding a banquet to celebrate Horus there. Father even sent the treasure of one of the past Pharaohs to show as an exhibit."

"Oh. I see."

"Don't worry, the treasure has been checked for any curses, it's not going to cause any problems."

"I'm glad." That they've thought to check it for

curses. I'm somewhat horrified that they think it's acceptable to dig up the treasure someone was buried with. I understand that it's important to learn from the past, but it feels like an affront to the gods to disturb someone's final resting place, especially one belonging to a Pharaoh.

But I'm not in a position to say anything about that. In all likelihood, I never will be. Even Nik's father would have problems speaking up about it. He may be the High Priest of Anubis here in the British Isles, but in terms of the empire, he has a lot less power than many of the other High Priests.

Not that I think I'll ever become a High Priestess of Anubis. As far as I'm aware, it isn't possible for a member of the Blessed to become a High Priest in the Temple of Anubis, which doesn't fully make sense when some other temples only ever have Blessed High Priests.

The vehicle comes to a stop and the door swings open. Ramesses jumps down before offering me his hand to help me do the same. I'm glad for his offer, getting in and out of the car wearing a dress like mine is particularly difficult.

He offers me his elbow and I slip my arm through his, placing my hand against his bare skin. The contact feels a little alien, but I push the feeling to the side. I need to focus on the impression I'm giving and not on what I'm thinking on the inside.

Yet another reason I wouldn't want to be a High Priestess even if I could be. I very much doubt I'd be any good at all of the social events needed for the position.

Ramesses exchanges pleasantries with several people as we make our way inside, but he doesn't bother introducing me to any of them. I'm not sure whether it's me he deems unworthy of the introduction, or them, but I'm not about to ask and risk finding out.

The moment we enter the museum, I'm captivated by the displays around me. Despite the fact I grew up not far from here, I've never actually been.

"Would you mind if we go to look at the exhibit first?" I ask. I may have my reservations about having grave goods on display, but I'm also intrigued to see them. Perhaps there'll be something to learn from them.

"Of course," Ramesses responds, steering me over in that direction.

I'm marginally surprised. I thought he'd take some more convincing, but apparently not.

He continues to greet people as we pass, but it

doesn't slow us down and we soon arrive at the exhibit he'd talked about in the car.

Glass cases stretch around the room, with glittering gold and intricate paintings displayed within.

"What do you want to look at?" he asks, seeming genuinely interested.

"All of it."

"I should have known you'd be interested in the dead."

"The dead are my life," I point out. "I'd be worried if I wasn't interested."

"I suppose." He lets go of me and I make my way around the room, checking out each of the items.

I come to a stop in front of a beautifully inlaid Senet board with ivory pieces. Even through the glass, the craftsmanship is exquisite.

"Do you know how to play?" Ramesses asks as he comes to stand beside me.

I nod. "I learned as a kid. What about you?"

"Of course. Though I prefer Hounds and Jackals as a game."

"I was never a huge fan of it," I admit.

"Maybe I can change your mind."

"Perhaps you can," I agree, surprised that he's thinking about something as relaxing as spending an evening playing board games. "Though I'm out of practice."

"Is there no one to play against at the temple?"

"I rarely find the time," I admit. Though perhaps I should make some. I've never asked Nik if he plays Senet. I imagine he does. Knowing the way his mind works, I imagine he's pretty good at it.

I'll ask if I get home before he goes to bed.

"We'll have to change that," Ramesses says.

I raise an eyebrow but don't point out that he's the main reason why I don't have time for things like that.

"You might need to tell me what all of these amulets mean," Ramesses says as he stops in front of a shallow case.

I make my way over and come to a stop beside him. "They're amulets from the body," I whisper, horrified that they've taken them away from where they belong. "This one is a heart scarab." I point to an oval-domed amulet sitting in the middle of the case.

"What's it for?"

I glance at him from the corner of my eye, wondering if he's seriously asking, or if he's just asking to keep me talking.

From the expression on his face, he really has no idea what any of the items in the case are.

"It helps bind the heart into silence while it's weighed against the feather of Ma'at in the Hall of Judgement."

"Silence doesn't sound like a good thing," Ramesses observes.

"I think it's so things don't get confused and your heart is weighed honestly." I shrug. "I can't pretend to know much more about it. That kind of question is for a priestess of Ma'at."

"That's a shame, I try to avoid them at all costs."

I let out a small laugh. "They are rather intimidating."

"I didn't realise you'd come across them."

I nod. "Nik and I had to give our testimonies over everything that happened with the organ theft."

A slight growl escaped from Ramesses, though I'm not sure which part of my statement it was aimed at.

"They asked me some questions, I answered them, and then they let me go home."

"And they did the same for Nikare?" There's an

edge to his voice that makes me think his growl was aimed at my fellow apprentice.

"That's what he said." And I have no reason to think it wasn't the case.

"Interesting."

I narrow my eyes but decide against prying more into whatever is going on between Ramesses and Nik. I wasn't even aware they knew one another.

But it's something I'm more comfortable asking Nik about than Ramesses, so he's the one I'm going to save my questions for.

A loud gong reverberates around the museum, calling us all to dinner.

"If you'll allow me to escort you to our seats?" Ramesses asks.

"I'd be delighted." Especially as the rumble of hunger has set in, and the food will no doubt be delicious. It always is.

But none of that changes the fact there's a large part of me that wishes I was at home with Nik and Matia.

Not that I'm ever going to admit that to anyone here.

Chapter 9

I cover my mouth before the yawn takes hold. Maybe I need to put in a request for some holiday so I can spend a few days in my room sleeping and finally shaking the exhaustion that's been plaguing me for weeks. I could even go back to my parents' house for it so no one could bother me even if they wanted to.

But that would mean leaving the temple, and there's a part of me that doesn't want to do that, even if it's only temporary.

"Another late night?" Nik whispers.

"You know it," I mutter.

"I do. I waited up as long as I could, but I need my beauty sleep."

"Then you need some more," I throw back at him.

He makes a shocked sound and presses his hands against his chest. "You wound me, Ani."

"Sure I do." I doubt anything can dent his self-confidence. And it's well deserved. Nik *is* easy on the eyes with his tanned skin and dark hair. He's the perfect example of what our society describes as handsome, and I'm not about to disagree with that.

Wait, why am I thinking about him like that? I don't look at Neffie that way despite the fact she's beautiful.

I push the thoughts aside and focus on making my way to the mortuary along with the rest of the apprentices.

Hannu sidles up to Nik, a worried expression on his face. It takes me a moment to realise he has no idea if Nik managed to replace the amulet last night. It's strange to think that was only half a day ago, it feels like so much has happened since then.

"Did you manage to make the switch?" Hannu whispers.

"I did," Nik promises.

"I..."

Nik shakes his head before I can confirm he did it.

I frown, but stay silent. I'll ask him about it once Hannu has returned to Ibi's side.

Hannu breathes a sigh of relief. "Thanks, Nik."

"Any time," my friend replies.

Hannu flashes him a tight smile and then drops back a few paces.

"Why didn't you let me tell him I'd seen you do it?" I ask, being careful not to let anyone overhear me.

"I don't want you to get into trouble if the body is still missing."

My heart swells. What a sweet thing for him to do.

"Do you really think there's a chance it isn't?"

Nik shakes his head. "I don't know how it would have miraculously turned up again. I doubt anyone who took it was just borrowing it."

"That's a somewhat disturbing image," I mutter. "What would they be doing with it for an evening?"

The expression Nik throws me answers my question.

"Oh. Ew."

He shrugs. "It used to be a much bigger problem than it is now."

"I'm glad it stopped."

"Apparently, people with very beautiful wives

used to make sure their bodies decomposed a bit before sending them to the mortuary temples just in case."

I wrinkle my nose. "There are so many things wrong with that statement."

"Wrong, but not inaccurate."

I snort. "How do you know so much about necrophilia?"

"I grew up here, I'd be more worried if I didn't know."

"Okay, so we're going to hope that Hannu's body was stolen by a necrophiliac and returned before this morning then?" A shiver runs down my spine. "That doesn't seem like a good thing for his chances of passing."

"It's not so great, no," Nik admits. "But the alternative is no body at all and that's a huge issue."

"What if the family notices?" Horror creeps through me. They'd be devastated.

"They won't," Nik assures me. "I doubt they'd let us do our mummification tests on a body the family want to see."

"Mildly reassuring," I mutter.

"But not particularly."

"Mmhmm."

Our conversation is ended by our arrival at the

mortuary. We make our way inside along with Hannu, Ibi, and the others. Nervous energy hangs in the air around us. Despite being confident in my own abilities, I'm as nervous as everyone else. But I'm not just nervous for me, I'm nervous for the rest of the apprentices. I want everyone to pass, even those I don't know very well.

Mostly, I'm worried about Hannu. I like the other apprentice, he's always been nice to me and he's good at our job. I don't want him to lose his place at the temple because someone stole his body.

And I don't want him to blame Nik for the disappearance either. I wish Nik had let me say I was there, it would be a defence for him if things go badly.

"Good morning, everyone," Hori says as we fall into neat lines in front of him. "I hope you all slept well."

I glance around the other faces. It doesn't appear that anyone had enough sleep, so at least I'm not alone, though I suspect their lack of sleep comes from a different place to mine.

"Congratulations, everybody passed," Hori announces. "The assessors were particularly impressed with your performances."

I turn to Nik to find my own shock mirrored on

his face. At least I'm not the only one who thinks it's a strange turn of events.

"Everyone passed?" Hannu echoes, hope in his voice.

"Yes," Hori confirms. "I'm very pleased with the results, but not surprised. As a reward, you're all being awarded the rest of the day off."

Excited chatter fills the room as the news sinks in.

I don't say anything. There's only one question I want the answer to, and I don't think here is the right place to voice it.

"You're dismissed. I'll see you bright and early tomorrow morning," Hori says, waving us all away.

"Do you want to take Matia for a walk?" Nik asks loud enough for the others to hear.

"I'll go get her." It isn't long since I took her out for her morning stretch, but I know she'll love having a second chance to go out, especially if it means she gets to play with Nik.

I'm looking forward to a more leisurely walk too, I feel like I've been letting Matia down with the amount of time I've spent with her.

"Should I meet you by the lake?" he asks.

"I'll be back in a few minutes."

I hurry back to the living quarters and up the stairs to collect Matia.

She's waiting by the door before I've even opened it, and I have to wonder whether this is to do with the bond Khafre has been trying to help me forge with her. It's hard to tell whether or not it's working, but I don't mind.

"Come on, girl, we're going to go play by the lake," I say as I pat my leg.

Matia lets out a yip and bounces out of my room. She hurries by my side as we make our way back down.

Nik waves me over to one of the benches, but it isn't until I get closer that I notice the pile of sticks by his feet.

A small smile lifts the corners of my lips. Matia is going to have such a good time.

I sit next to him and lean back. I close my eyes and enjoy the early morning sun.

"I don't know why they didn't tell us they were going to give us the day off before," Nik muses.

"You're telling me. I could have done with more sleep," I admit.

"Has Ramesses been keeping you up all night again?" There's a bitter tone in his voice that's hard to ignore.

"What's your problem with him?" I ask, more interested than insulted.

He sighs. "Nothing, really."

"Why am I not convinced?"

He chuckles. "I can't explain it," he admits. "You know when you just meet someone and you don't like them but can't explain why?"

I nod.

"That's what it's like with Ramesses. We've met a few times over the years and we've just never clicked. I'm reasonably sure the feeling is mutual."

"I am too, if that helps." Though I'm also certain there's more to it, but if Nik isn't ready to tell me what it is, I'm not going to push him on it.

"It does, actually." He sighs. "But I don't dislike him that much. So long as you're happy."

"Thanks, Nik." It's weird to be talking about things like this with him, especially when he doesn't like Ramesses. But with Neffie busy at Bastet's temple, I'll take what I can get.

We lapse into a comfortable silence as Matia chases after a stick Nik has thrown for her.

"What's going on with Hannu's body?" I ask.

"I have no idea. Maybe we're right and it was just a necrophilia thing."

I wrinkle my nose. "That's still not a good thing," I point out.

"True. But it's better than a missing body."

"Maybe? I'm not so sure." A shiver runs down my spine as I think about the potential consequences of that.

"We could investigate," he suggests.

"No." The word comes out more forcefully than I intend it to.

Nik turns to face me, surprise written all over his expression.

"I want to get to the bottom of it as much as you do," I admit. "But we can't risk getting into more trouble."

"We won't," he responds.

"Just like we weren't going to last time?"

He sighs. "You may have a point."

"There's no may about it, I *do* have a point. We got into a lot of trouble for interfering in temple business and putting ourselves at risk, we shouldn't do that again."

Indecision wars over his face. "So what are you suggesting?"

"I don't know. But I don't think we should rush into anything." Even as I say it, I realise I hate it. I don't want to just sit by while bad things happen, but I'm not sure what else to do.

Nik sighs. "We should still keep an eye out for anything else strange."

"Always," I agree.

We let the conversation fall away and focus on playing with Matia. It's nice to have some time off and not have to think of anything important. I wish I had more moments like this.

Chapter 10

"Are you sure Matia is allowed in here?" I ask Khafre. "They normally ban her from the mortuary." And with good reason. I love Matia dearly, but there's no changing the fact she's a jackal, bringing a scavenger around dead bodies doesn't seem like the smartest move.

"It'll be fine," Khafre promises. "Your bond with her is sufficient to keep her from doing anything."

I glance at my jackal. She cocks her head to the side and stares at me as if to promise she won't misbehave. I want to believe her, especially as I've never had her in here to know how she normally is.

"I don't feel like our bond has changed very much," I admit.

Khafre nods. "That makes sense, yours is one of

the stronger ones I've seen at the beginning of the bonding process. I suspect it's the extra time you had at the beginning without me. You must have started it without realising."

"Oh." I suppose that makes sense. Matia has always been well-behaved, perhaps this is why.

"You have to trust her or your bond won't be sustainable," Khafre says.

"I do." I reach out and scratch Matia's head, hoping it lets her know how true my words are. She leans into my hand, whether because of my sentiments, or because I'm hitting just the right spot, I'm not sure, but I suppose it doesn't matter.

"All right, now we've sorted that out, we're going to start our lesson. Are you ready?"

I nod. "Why are we not in the hall we normally use?" I ask.

"You'll see."

I frown. Why is he suddenly being so cryptic? If there's one thing I particularly appreciate about Khafre, it's that he doesn't do the whole confusingly cryptic thing. He always explains the things we're doing. I like that he never makes me feel as if he's excluding me from my training.

Which means there's going to be a reason for what hc's doing today.

He pushes the door in front of us open and I'm immediately hit by the stench of rotting.

"Sorry, there's no real way to prepare you for this bit," he says as we step inside.

"I've never been in here before," I admit.

"You might have. It doesn't always contain body parts," he says, gesturing towards the table.

"That's a relief," I mutter. I have no idea what we're doing here, but hopefully, we can be done quickly so I can get out of here and have the hottest shower I can manage.

"I'm sure you've learned about noticing the signs of decomposition from the outside," Khafre says.

"And inside."

He chuckles. "Well yes, I meant including inside the body cavities."

"It's one of the first things Hori and Addaya taught us."

"Ah, yes, Addaya is particularly adept at it. He entered the priesthood later than most and was training to be a doctor before."

My eyebrows shoot up. I had no idea of that. Addaya may be one of our supervisors, but he has less to do with us than Hori does.

"Anyway, one of the skills you have as someone

Blessed by Anubis is to sense decay in a different way."

"Another way?"

He nods. "I hope you don't have anything against getting your hands dirty."

"I've been studying embalming for months."

Khafre gives a jovial laugh. "Good point." He leads me over to an amputated arm.

"Where have these all come from?" I ask.

"Some are from the Heka's temple. I believe the arm belongs to a blacksmith's apprentice who had an accident."

I wince. "Ouch."

"My thoughts exactly," Khafre agrees. "Some of the organs are from the traditional mummification rooms, but only the ones that aren't necessary. The rest comes from criminals who have been denied the mummification process as part of their punishment."

I stare down at the body parts, feeling conflicted about it all. "Right."

"Everything is above board with asking permission," he promises. "Even from the criminals."

"Okay, that's good." I think. I'm not really sure what to make of it all.

"But we're getting off track. Right now, we're

supposed to be focusing on having you identify decay."

"How are we going to do that?" I ask.

"We're going to start with the arm. What can you tell me from how it looks?"

"Can I touch it?" I ask.

"Yes, but don't turn it over."

"Why?"

"Because that would destroy my lesson."

Ah. That's a good reason not to.

I head over to the sink and scrub my hands vigorously. I check them for cuts and abrasions as I do. The last thing I want is to get an infection, though I doubt Khafre has brought anything contagious. I don't think the doctors at Heka's temple would let him take anything they thought would cause illness in someone else. Their worship is too based on people's health for them to risk that.

Besides, I doubt they want more work on their hands.

I move back to the arm and study it closely from every angle.

"I'd say this was removed from the body less than a day ago," I say. "There are very few signs of decomposition and no skin slippage, which makes it unlikely it was longer."

"Excellent. You're right, by the way. It was amputated first thing this morning. Now I want you to close your eyes and place your hand on the arm."

I do as instructed, even if a part of me is worried about the somewhat strange lesson he's taking me through.

"Take a deep breath."

"Even with the smell?"

Khafre chuckles. "There's no getting around that, I'm afraid. But you need to centre yourself so you can focus on your bond with Anubis."

The smell isn't as bad as I expect it to be. I'm probably getting used to it.

"What can you feel?" he asks.

"It just feels like an arm."

"Okay, that's a good start."

"What do I do now?" I want to get this right.

"Focus," he instructs. "Think about what you expect to feel when you touch your own arm, and then compare it to what's in this one."

I direct all of my attention to the cold limb on the table in front of me. At first, I can't sense anything, but after a moment, something snaps.

"I can feel it," I whisper.

"Okay, good. But what exactly can you feel?"

I frown. Why is he asking when I already made

my visual assessment? He said I was right about the amount of time since the arm's amputation.

But he also specifically said I wasn't to turn the arm over because it would ruin the lesson, which has to mean that there's something more to this than what I first saw.

I take another breath and hone in on the arm, trying to work out what I'm missing.

Khafre doesn't say anything, which I assume means I'm doing what he expects me to.

Reassured, I continue.

Matia leans her head against my leg and I reach down and touch my free hand to her head.

Something snaps into place and I gain a greater sense of what's going on with the arm in front of me. I can't locate the exact points of the decomposition process, but I feel like I can sense more about what stage the arm as a whole is in.

"There's something strange about it," I say out loud. "Like a part of the arm is more decomposed than the rest."

"Very good." It's impossible to miss the satisfaction in Khafre's voice. I'm not sure if it's because I've successfully managed to do what he's teaching me to, or because I'm right. "You can open your eyes now."

"What is it?" I ask.

"Turn the arm over," he instructs.

Intrigued, I roll it over and let out a small gasp. A gaping wound sits on the other side with all of the signs of an inflamed infection. I may not be trained in medicine like Heka's priests, but I know enough to be able to tell that this would have been incredibly uncomfortable for the blacksmith's apprentice.

"What you were sensing is that the infection had caused some of the flesh to start decomposing even before the arm was amputated."

"And that's why the priests took such a drastic course of action?" I ask.

He nods. "It was too far gone and was starting to cause blood poisoning. If Heka's priests hadn't acted when they did, we'd have his entire body and not just his arm."

I nod.

"All right, your next task is to sort the body parts in order of most decomposed to least."

I wrinkle my nose, causing Khafre to laugh.

"I know, it's horrible, but there's no better way to learn this than by trying to be hands-on."

I let out a loud sigh. "I can see that." And I'll be doing whatever he says regardless of how disgusting a task sounds. He knows what he's talking about when it comes to being Blessed, and I'm here to learn from him no matter what that means for my nose.

With Matia by my side, I start touching each of the body parts in turn and start sorting them into some kind of order. I may not get it right the first time, but so long as I learn as I go, I don't think that's a problem.

Luckily for me, Khafre is a patient teacher and I don't think I have to worry about him getting annoyed at me for taking so long. If it's ever my turn to mentor a new Blessed, I'm going to remember what he did for me and make sure I act the same way towards my trainee.

Especially if this does teach me what I need to know.

Chapter 11

The pinch of my headdress is almost impossible to ignore, especially with how hot the room is getting. As if I need more reasons to not want to be at fancy banquets, being uncomfortable is definitely making it all worse.

"Why don't you have some more wine?" Ramesses suggests, already filling up my goblet.

I consider telling him no, but it's going to be easier to just not drink it. I've had enough, especially considering I'm supposed to be in the mortuary tomorrow morning.

"Are you having a good time?" he asks.

I nod. "The food is delicious." That's not a lie. It has to be some of the best I've had served to me at one of these events. Which says a lot when I've been attending them with Ramesses. All of the hosts are trying to serve the best while they have a prince amongst their guests.

"Have you tried the beer? They had it imported from Egypt." He hands me another glass, as if drinking more alcohol is a good idea.

"I haven't, no." I take it from him and sip slowly. There's no getting around this one. "It's delicious. It's a lot better than the beer they brew here."

He chuckles. "You're not wrong there."

"How long are you staying in the British Isles?" I ask.

He shrugs. "Until I have a reason to leave." Something in the way he looks at me suggests that has something to do with me. But I doubt it. We're only just getting to know one another properly. While all of the dates he's been taking me on are still banquets and formal events, something seems to have changed between us since our trip to the museum. It finally feels as if Ramesses is interested in talking to me and not just turning up with me on his arm.

"Do you miss it?" I ask.

"Egypt?"

I nod. "You've been gone for a few months."

"I've been travelling my whole life. I've probably

spent more time away from Egypt than I have living in the palace."

"That doesn't mean you can't miss it," I point out.

"Maybe not." He sighs and takes a big drink of wine. "There's nothing much for me to do there anyway. My sister has most of the responsibility as my father's chosen heir."

"What's she like?" I've only ever heard rumours about Princess Iset. I wouldn't mind meeting her. It's not the first time a Pharaoh has chosen a daughter to inherit, but it doesn't happen very often, and not when there's an adult son.

"Can we not talk about my sister?" Ramesses asks, a dark tone in his voice.

I should have known that the succession was something he wouldn't want brought up. "Of course, I'm sorry."

"No need to be. Why don't we take a walk?" he suggests. "I've heard there are some beautiful wall paintings in the courtyards here."

"I'd like that," I answer honestly. It'll give me a chance to clear my head from the combination of wine and the heat in the room, as well as allow me to talk to Ramesses in private. Those are always the best conversations.

He gets to his feet and holds out his arm for me to take. The moment I place my hand against his skin, he covers it with his own in a way that could be seen as affectionate to anyone watching. As it is, I don't think anyone is paying us much attention.

I let out a relieved sigh as we leave the oppressive air of the banquet hall. The cool breeze coming from outside is a welcome change, even if it does chill me a little more than necessary.

We come to a stop in front of a huge mural painted in exquisite detail.

"It's beautiful," I say.

"It is," Ramesses agrees. "It's not all done in the traditional style. The original owners of the house wanted to incorporate some of the ancient traditions of the locals." He points to a black dog-like figure with red eyes.

"That's not one of Anubis' jackals."

"It's not," Ramesses agrees. "Mother told me about this wall when I was ten. She said that it depicts the legend of the black dog. He's supposed to be a harbinger of doom to those who cross his path. It's a legend that used to be popular in the moorlands before the British Isles became part of the Empire."

"I've never heard the legend before."

"I'm not surprised. A lot of the local legends have disappeared."

"Isn't that sad to think about sometimes?" I ask. "The Empire has taken over so many countries and erased part of their history."

Ramesses shrugs. "It's a small price to pay for being part of an Empire that has the most advanced medicine and technology available. People come from all over the world to take advantage of that."

"True." I should know better than to question the Empire in front of a member of the royal family. It's not like I even have a problem with it. This is the world I've grown up in my entire life, and there are a lot of advantages beyond just the technology and healthcare. I don't have to worry about being made a slave, I can travel to anywhere in the Empire without much trouble, and none of the people living within the Empire's borders have to worry about things like famine or drought. The Empire looks out for those who live within its borders, it always has done.

And I wouldn't forsake Anubis and my chance to serve him for anything. I've found my purpose in life at the temple. Maybe that will change as I grow older, but if it does, then I'll find my new purpose.

No one is going to hold me to a decision I made at eighteen.

Ramesses moves me away from the wall painting and into a room made of glass. A large pool sits in the middle of it, with lotus blossoms jutting from the top of it and small fish swimming around lazily beneath the surface.

"Shall we sit?" Ramesses asks, gesturing to a dip in the side of the pool that seems to have been designed for just that.

I glance at the entrance. "Are we allowed in here?"

"I'm the prince of the entire empire, I can do whatever I want."

I smile, but it feels forced. I don't think his position should give him the right to do anything he wants, but I know I'm not going to change his mind about that.

And the water does look wonderfully inviting.

I slip off my sandals and hitch up my dress so I can step onto the seat without getting it wet. Perhaps another lady wouldn't care, but I only have a handful of formal dresses and I don't want to risk ruining one of them.

The water is cool against my feet, and the pleasing scent of the lotuses fills the air as they're stirred by our presence. The fish scatter at first, but don't stay away for long. They return and start nibbling at my feet, causing me to giggle softly.

"It smells much better than the mortuary in here," I admit.

"I imagine most things do."

"True. But you get used to it after a while." The mortuary smell has almost become comforting to me now.

I swish my feet through the water, enjoying the way it feels between my toes.

"Ani."

I turn to face him, unsure what he needs my attention for.

Ramesses leans in, his face barely more than a few inches from mine. Is he going to kiss me? I'm not sure how I feel about that.

The wine from dinner is still making my head a bit dizzy, which I don't think is the best thing for it to be when there's a potential first kiss involved.

Ramesses closes the distance and presses his lips against mine.

I push on his chest and lean back, not wanting this to go any further.

Discontent flashes over his face, but he covers it quickly enough for me to doubt I've seen it.

"I'm sorry," I start, not sure what else I'm actually going to say.

"It's fine." His voice is surprisingly level, almost devoid of emotion completely.

"Ramesses..."

"It's fine," he repeats, getting to his feet and slipping his sandals back on. "We're expected back at the banquet," he says stiffly.

I blink a few times, trying to process what's happening. Is he angry at me for not wanting to kiss him? I don't want to rush into something like this when I've been drinking.

After a moment I nod and follow him to my feet. Hopefully, we'll get a chance to talk this through before things are too damaged between us to fix.

Chapter 12

I make my way to the amulet store with a list of what everyone needs. While I don't technically need to collect amulets for everyone, if I'm going for myself, it's just as easy to get others too.

Besides, I appreciate it when someone else does the same for me.

Vast baskets fill the room, each containing a different type of amulet in varying degrees of intricacy. The more someone pays for the mummification and burial process, the fancier the design of the amulets which get wrapped in the linen around their bodies. While some people do bring their own, most of the bodies we're dealing with as apprentices are those who choose the cheapest options.

I hum to myself as I add three heart scarabs to

my basket. When it comes time for my own burial, I think I want a heart scarab that's made just for me, but maybe that will change with the more time I spend in the temple learning about how things work. I'm fully aware that I may change my mind at some point.

Once I'm done, I head back to the main mortuary room, satisfied that I've got everything my fellow apprentices asked for. We're just preparing bodies today rather than learning anything new, so I don't mind being away from the one that's been assigned to me. I doubt any of the others would let anything happen to it. I never imagined we'd end up feeling as much like a team as we do, but I'm certainly not complaining about it. I like it.

"Thanks," I say to the priest holding the door open for me.

"You're welcome." He slips inside to collect his own amulets, which is surprising. Most of the priests higher up have assistants or scribes to do that for them. It turns out there are a lot of staff members in the temple who aren't part of the priesthood.

He probably just wants a moment to himself and this is the easiest way to get it. I'm not about to begrudge him that.

I weave through the mortuary tables, making sure I keep out of the way of anyone in the middle of a procedure.

"I'm surprised at how well the girl apprentice is doing," an older guy with his back to me says to his friend.

"She's only here because she's shacking up with the prince," the second apprentice responds. "I don't pay any attention to how she's doing."

The first man chortles. "You might have a point there. Though I thought it was the High Priest's son she was into. Maybe she's playing both of them."

My blood runs cold and tears prick at my eyes. I blink them away, not wanting anyone to see they're getting me.

I ignore the two men and head towards Hannu and Ibi to set down their amulets before moving on to Djou and Ahmes.

"Where's Nik?" I ask as I set his amulets down next to his station.

"He's gone to get some more linen," Djou answers. "Some of the stuff we got earlier is too discoloured to use on these bodies." He points to the neatly folded pile at the end of the bench.

"Ah, thanks." I move back to my table and place the nearly empty basket down on the end of it.

I stare at the dead woman's unblinking face, knowing I need to start wrapping her, but unable to move. All I can do is think about the way the older apprentices are talking about me. Do people really think I'm only here because I'm dating Ramesses? I didn't even meet the prince until after I'd started my apprenticeship here. He couldn't have given me this even if he wanted to.

"Ani, are you all right?" Hannu asks.

I shake my head and turn away, rushing back through the mortuary without stopping, even for a moment. I need to get some air or I'm going to end up bursting into tears, which isn't going to help my reputation with anyone in the temple.

I push through the front door of the mortuary, not paying any attention to where I'm going until I realise I've come to the bench Nik and I often come to when we want to play with Matia.

I sit down and hide my head in my hands, taking deep shaking breaths as I try to keep the tears at bay.

Footsteps sound from behind me.

"Go away." I don't know who it is, and I might regret it later when one of my superiors tells me off for it, but right now, I don't want to be around people.

"Not until you tell me what's wrong." There's a hint of concern in Nik's voice, but maybe I'm imagining it. "Ani..."

I sigh and look up.

"Do you want to talk about it, or do you want to just sit here?"

"You should go back inside. Don't get in trouble on my account," I mumble. I want him to stay, but I don't want him to damage his standing here at the same time.

"What's the use of being the High Priest's son if I can't pull some strings."

I raise an eyebrow. "I thought you weren't going to use that line anymore?"

"Only when it comes to the people I care about."

My traitorous heart flutters at his words. It's silly, I know Nik cares about me, he's made it clear on numerous occasions that he thinks of us as friends. And I do too.

"Do you want to talk about it?"

"No."

"I'm a good listener."

I let out a loud sigh. "I know you are. But I can't talk to anyone about this. Except maybe Neffie, but she's not here." Frustration slips into my voice.

"You really miss her," he observes.

"She's my best friend. Don't you miss yours?"

He fiddles with his hands, not meeting my gaze.

"You don't have a best friend, do you?"

"I do," he counters. "But I've never had one before you."

"Oh. Sorry."

He shrugs. "Don't be. It's my own fault. When I was growing up, I always assumed people thought the worst of me because of who my father was."

"You don't really do anything to prove them otherwise," I point out. "You can tend to be a bit arrogant about it."

"I know. It's not purposeful. But you're the first person to see past that. And now the rest of our group do too."

"That's because you let them see who you really are," I point out. "You helped with Hannu and the amulet, and you don't try and steal the attention of the room."

"I think they like me because they like you," he counters.

"I don't think any of them are that shallow," I point out.

He sighs. "Maybe. But we're not here to talk

about my previous lack of best friend. What happened to make you run out of there?"

"I don't want to talk about it."

"Not even if I pretend to be Neffie?"

I stare at him with a disbelieving look on my face.

He clears his throat. "Hello, I'm Neffie," he says in a squeaky voice. "I'm a priestess for Bastet and I've known you your entire life."

Without meaning to, I let out a small laugh.

"She would kill you if she ever found out about this."

"I don't think so," Nik says as he continues to do a terrible imitation of my best friend. "She'd say that it was worth it to see you smile."

I laugh again, doing just what he wants without even meaning to. "I still don't want to talk about it."

"That's okay," he says in his normal voice. "I can distract you in other ways. I could tell you what I've discovered about the missing bodies."

"Nik! You weren't supposed to investigate more."

"What? I didn't get you into trouble."

"It's not me I'm worried about. I don't want you getting into more trouble either."

"I was careful."

I sigh. "Fine. Tell me what else you found."

"Nothing concrete. I found three more missing bodies, but they have nothing in common other than being dead."

"That's reassuring considering what they're here for," I mutter. "But nothing at all?"

"No. All three of these bodies, plus the one Hannu embalmed, were all different ages, different causes of death, and three were men while one was a woman."

I sigh. "Any correlation between who embalmed them?"

"None at all. I didn't even recognise the names of two of them."

"That's not particularly helpful."

"No, it isn't."

"You should tell your father about this," I say.

Shock travels over his features. "I can't."

"You have to. Clearly something is going on, and you don't know what it is. If your father finds out you've been investigating again, he's not going to be very happy. You can't risk that."

He purses his lips, clearly not happy with what I'm suggesting. "All right, I'll tell my father. But you have to come with me when I do."

"Me?" I raise an eyebrow.

"If I'm telling him because you want me to, then yes, you're definitely coming with me."

"You know I'll be there."

"I do." He grins. "Feeling better?"

"I am, thank you." And I mean it. I suspect I'm still going to have to deal with the repercussions of what I overheard the older apprentices talking about, but Nik has reminded me I don't have to deal with it alone. I have him, and I have the rest of the junior apprentices too.

"Are you ready to go back in?" he asks.

I sigh. "No. But I also know I have to. I have a Blessed lesson this afternoon too."

"Then I guess telling my father about the missing bodies will have to wait until tomorrow."

"Don't think I'm going to change my mind overnight."

He holds his hands up defensively. "I didn't think you would."

"Good. Now come on, let's get back to work." I get up and start heading back towards the mortuary with Nik in tow.

Chapter 13

I push open the door to the room where Khafre taught me about sensing decay with only a small amount of nerves about what he wants me to do today. I don't think it can get much worse than before. Some of the decomposed body parts were so far gone it took me days to stop smelling them.

Matia jumps along beside me, happy to be allowed inside the mortuary again. She's still not allowed to join me while I'm performing my normal duties, but it seems that my Blessed lessons are different. Presumably, when I start having duties as one of Anubis' Blessed she'll be allowed to come too. Which is a relief, I always feel guilty when I shut my bedroom door on her during the day. It would be much easier if she enjoyed spending time with the other jackals, but something about belonging to a member of the Blessed seems to have made it so she doesn't like it.

"Good afternoon, Ani," Khafre says brightly.

Beni rushes forward and nuzzles into Matia with her snout. To my surprise, my jackal responds in kind, seeming to like the affection.

Maybe it really is something about being attached to someone Blessed that's changed how she views the world.

"Hey," I say. "It doesn't smell today."

Khafre chuckles. "No, it doesn't. Today's lesson doesn't involve as much mess."

"I'm glad, I heard the priest assigned to clearing it up complaining for several days."

"I'm not sure I blame him, it's not the best task to be assigned."

"So, what are we doing today?"

"You're going to be telling me which method of mummification was used on each of these bodies." He waves to four linen-wrapped cadavers.

"I can do that?"

He nods. "You should be able to."

"How is that useful?" I can see how being able to sense decay has its uses, especially when preparing a difficult body. Sometimes, it's important to know what needs the most treatment so we can focus on that first.

"That's a good question. Unfortunately, some-times mix-ups and clerical errors can happen, this is one of the ways it can be sorted out."

"You mean if a body is supposed to have under-gone traditional mummification but went through modern embalming instead, then we can tell it's not in the right coffin?"

"Precisely that. Obviously, it's better if that doesn't happen. But when there are people involved, things like that are inevitable to some extent. We're the last line of defence against that."

"That makes sense." I think.

"And there are some other more practical applications of the gift, particularly around cere-monies such as the opening of the mouth, but I'll teach you those later."

"I'll be doing that?"

"Once you reach the seniority to, yes," Khafre responds. "Right now, it's unlikely you'll be performing any of the rituals."

"Right, got it." I'm not expecting any special treatment because I'm Blessed. Beyond the fact I'm currently having lessons that no one else is, I mean.

"Do you remember how you were able to sense decay?" Khafre asks.

I nod.

"Good. The theory is similar. Why not come over to the first body." He gestures to the closest linen-wrapped body.

I move over to stand next to it, Matia still by my side. I reach out, but then hesitate, unsure whether or not it's right to treat the body this way.

"We have permission," Khafre assures me.

"How..."

"I had the same question when my Blessed mentor took me through this lesson. I imagine you're thinking that it goes against what you've been taught."

"Yes."

"Luckily, you seem to be picking up things quickly, so you don't have to do this part for very long. But the families of the deceased know that they're helping the Blessed," he says.

"Why do they do it?"

"The same reason people accept embalming services from apprentices," he admits. "It makes things cheaper for them."

"Oh."

"For one of these bodies, it meant an upgrade

from modern embalming to traditional mummifica-tion. I'm sure you know enough to understand how desirable that is."

"I do." A lot of people want the traditional method but discover they can't afford it. That's one of the reasons the temple of Anubis developed modern embalming. A cheaper option makes mummification more accessible to everyone.

"When you're ready, place your hand on the deceased and search out for it, like you did with the arm," Khafre instructs.

I place one hand at my side and wait for Matia to press her head against it before placing my other on top of the mummy's head. Khafre seems to be able to do this kind of thing without Beni's help, but I suspect that's only because he's had longer to prac-tise. For now, I need to stick with taking Matia's assistance.

I close my eyes and take a deep breath. The room smells ever so slightly of chemicals, but that doesn't mean they're coming from this body. I push past them and focus on what I can feel beneath my hands instead.

The linen isn't the best quality, but that is irrele-vant at the moment. Underneath that, there's a sensation of dryness, though I'm not sure what that means.

Unless...

"This person was traditionally mummified," I say, my voice shaking.

"Very good. I'm impressed you were able to ignore the chemical smells to pick up on that."

"They were meant to distract me?"

"I'm sorry, but yes. It's the only way to know for sure whether a student is just guessing. Let's move on to the next one."

I take my time with the other two bodies, trying to get a feel for the way each type of embalming feels. It's easy to recognise the unnaturalness of modern embalming in the second body, but the third one has me more confused.

"It doesn't feel like this body has been embalmed at all," I say.

Khafre chuckles. "I told my teacher the exact same thing."

"Which means I'm wrong?"

"You are. This person was naturally mummified."

Understanding of what I sensed from the body rushes through me. "I mistook the natural feel for it not being embalmed."

"You did. But that's okay, a lot of people make the same mistake. That's part of the reason we train."

I appreciate that he's not trying to make me feel like an idiot for getting it wrong.

"All right, last one." He gestures to the final body.

I make my way over, sure this is going to be a repeat of one of the others. Unless there's some new mummification technique that I don't know about, which is perfectly possible given I've been here less than a year.

I place my hand on top of the body and search through it the same way I have with all of the others.

My eyebrows knit together into a frown as I try to make sense of what I'm feeling from it.

I hesitate for a moment, unsure if I want to voice what I think, or if I'm just projecting my discovery with Nik. "I don't think there's a body in here."

"I'm impressed, most people don't get that one."

"It's always used as a test?"

"Of course, it's important that Blessed can recognise when there's no body."

My curiosity is piqued. "Does that happen often?"

"I've never seen it in real life," Khafre admits. "Just when one of the Blessed needs a dummy like this for practice."

"Oh."

"You seem disappointed. Is there anything on your mind?"

A small part of me wants to ask him more about fake bodies, but I can't without getting Nik into trouble. And probably me too. "Sorry, it's nothing," I dismiss.

He nods. "I understand. If you change your mind about what's bothering you, know that my door is always open."

"Thank you," I murmur, unsure how else to respond. But I can't talk to Khafre about this without checking with Nik first. We're going to do this the right way, which means keeping things quiet until we get a chance to talk to his father.

Even if there's a small chance Khafre might have the answers.

"I'm not sure what's bothering you, but if I may, I'd like to give you a piece of advice," Khafre says. "No matter what the situation is, trust your gut. That's the way Anubis likes to communicate with us. You'll start recognising it as your Blessed Sense when you get more used to it."

I manage a weak smile. "You make it sound so easy."

"It gets easier," he promises. "And luckily a lot of people don't think about asking us hard questions."

"That's a relief."

"Most of the time, people will completely forget you're Blessed. It doesn't make much of a difference to your day-to-day life as a priest. Well, priestess in your case." He flashes me a reassuring smile. "Anyway, that's all for today. I'll see you when we have our next lesson," he dismisses me.

Which I guess means it's time for me to go find Nik so we can prepare what to say to his father. There's no way I'm going into that meeting without a plan.

Chapter 14

"You need to calm down or you're going to wear a hole in the floor," Nik says from his seat in the hallway in front of his father's office.

"That's easy for you to say," I mutter. "You're used to this."

"Is it worth reminding you that this whole thing was your idea?"

"No."

"Then I'll refrain from saying so."

My lips quirk up into a mildly amused smile. "I appreciate it."

"It's going to be fine. Like you pointed out, we're doing exactly what Father asked us to do last time we were here," he says.

"Except that we discovered the first body doing

something he definitely wouldn't approve of," I remind him.

"Well, yes, but we're not going to say as much."

"And I have no idea how you found out about the others."

"I..."

I hold up my hand to stop him. "I'd rather not know. Keep it to yourself so I don't get us into trouble."

"If you insist."

"I do." I return to my pacing, not at all reassured by his attempts at calming me down. "I swear I'm more nervous than I was in the Hall of Ma'at."

"That's because this time you've done something wrong," he teases.

I stop my pacing and turn so I can glare at him.

"I'm sorry, it was right there, I couldn't stay silent."

"I'd tell you off for it, but we both know I'd have said the same thing," I admit.

He chuckles. "Are you feeling better after whatever happened in the morgue?" he asks, a more serious note taking over his voice.

"Yes. Mostly thanks to you." I sit down next to him and lean back against the wall.

"You're welcome. Did you manage to get hold

of Neffie to talk about whatever was bothering you?"

I nod. "We messaged last night after I left you. It's not as good as seeing her in person, but right now, it's as good as I can get."

"Do you have a day off together soon?"

"Only for the Tamesas festival."

"At least that's not far away."

"Mmhmm." Though I want to spend our time at the festival enjoying ourselves rather than talking about serious things like whether or not I actually want to kiss the guy I'm dating.

Then again, that is perfect girl talk.

The door to the High Priest's office creaks open and Nik's father steps through it. "Come in."

Nik and I get to our feet in unison. He reaches out and grabs my hand, giving it a reassuring squeeze. The gentle touch fills me with a warm glow that makes me feel as if I can deal with anything.

Including a meeting with his father.

"Sit down," High Priest Ahmose instructs.

I sit in one of the uncomfortable chairs on the visitor side of the desk, wishing it was longer since I was last here.

And that I was here for something better than

this. I've only ever had one conversation with the High Priest that wasn't about something bad.

"Dare I ask what the two of you are doing here?" he asks, his gaze flitting between us. "Given the last time the three of us were having a conversation, I can't imagine it's a good thing."

I exchange a glance with Nik and take a deep breath to steady my nerves. It's going to be fine. All I need to do is keep calm and be honest-ish about what's happened. So long as we omit the parts where we've broken the rules.

"We were doing some checks on the mummies for the mummification tests and we noticed something weird," I say, happy that we decided to stay as close to the truth as possible without getting anyone into trouble. The last thing we need is for Hannu to be retroactively failed because he forgot the amulet.

"Weird how?" he asks.

"The body had disappeared," Nik says. "We knew it was there because we saw one of the other apprentices preparing it properly, but when we checked, it was gone."

The High Priest raises an eyebrow. "Gone?"

I nod.

"I'm sure the mortuary clerks would have

noticed if there was a body missing," the High Priest says.

"It had been replaced by treated linen," I say. "And then the next day when the results were announced, everyone had passed. It didn't make sense when one of the bodies wasn't there."

"Which apprentice was it that prepared the body?"

"I don't remember," I lie. We can't get Hannu into trouble, especially when he has no idea of what's going on.

"Nik?"

He shakes his head. "I don't remember either, Father."

"Hmm." It's clear from the older man's face that he doesn't believe us, but thankfully he doesn't push it further. "And it was just this one body? Is there a chance you were mistaken about what happened?"

"There's no chance," Nik says. "I noticed first, and then I asked Ani to check." He flashes me a reassuring smile.

"I'm sorry to say that the word of two apprentices isn't going to go very far with an issue as serious as this," the High Priest says.

"We've found three other bodies missing since," Nik says, a note of panic in his voice. "We wouldn't have brought this to you if we didn't think there was a bigger problem at hand. But we've both kept an eye out for the same problems since, and found more."

"Hmm. Is there any correlation between them?"

"I'm not sure," Nik responds. "But we made sure to write all of the information we know down." He passes a sheet over to his father.

The High Priest takes it and scans it. "I'll look into this," he says. "And tomorrow, I want you to show me where you've found the missing bodies."

"You believe us?" I blurt.

The High Priest raises an eyebrow, presumably a little confused by my outburst. "I have no reason to think you'd lie to me. And while you went about it the wrong way last time, you were right about the organ thieves working out of the mortuary. I'm willing to take a chance that the two of you are right this time too."

Relief floods through me. I'm not sure what I expected, but somehow, the High Priest taking us seriously wasn't it.

"You're dismissed. I'll let you know the plan for tomorrow later." He sets down the sheet of paper on his pile and turns to deal with whatever is next on his list, effectively dismissing us.

"Thank you for hearing us out, Father," Nik says as he gets to his feet.

I echo the same sentiments and follow him out of the room.

The moment we're alone, I breathe a sigh of relief. "That went better than I expected."

"It did," Nik agrees. "I think that's the biggest compliment I've ever gotten from my father about my work."

"He doesn't think you're doing well?" I don't even try to keep the surprise out of my voice. Nik is one of the best apprentices amongst us, I don't understand how his father doesn't want to celebrate that.

"I don't think it's a matter of not thinking about it, I think it's just that he doesn't pay enough attention."

"Well I do, and I think you're doing great."

"Thanks, Ani." The way he says it makes me think he's actually grateful.

"We should get some lunch before we have to be back at the mortuary," I say.

He nods. "Good idea, I hate embalming on an empty stomach."

"I suspect a lot of people would find that weird," I tease.

"Then it's a good thing you're not a lot of people."

"I suppose if we were squeamish, we'd have bigger problems than what other people think" I muse.

"It's a good job I like being a little bit strange."

"Even if it ruins your reputation as a poster child?" I ask.

Nik chuckles. "I was always supposed to be a poster child for Anubis anyway. Having the ability to hold my lunch while faced with disgusting sights is an important part of the job."

I let out a snort. "You're not wrong."

He pushes open the door to the dining hall and gestures for me to step through.

I smile my gratitude towards him. Having a meeting with his father has meant we've got a little bit of time to ourselves.

"Do you want to play Senet?" I blurt.

Nik raises an eyebrow.

"We have a bit of time, and I realised I have no idea if you play."

"I do, but not often."

"So do you want to now?" I ask.

"You want to play a board game with me?" he checks.

"Is that not what friends do?" Is it weird for me to have asked him to do something like this? I don't think so, but maybe I've read the situation wrong.

"Sorry, I was just surprised. But we can grab something to eat and one of the boards so we can play."

I nod, eager to go up against him. I imagine his intelligence makes him a formidable opponent and I welcome the challenge.

Chapter 15

Despite the fact the High Priest has already said he believes us and is coming to look into things, I'm still nervous about it.

Most of the other priests and apprentices have already left for the day, but as soon as the High Priest gets here, they'll likely disappear.

I wipe down the already impeccable mortuary table. Volunteering for clean-up duty has made it all too easy to stay behind and avoid too many questions. No one wants clean-up duty. It's why it ended up being our punishment for stopping the organ-stealing ring by being reckless.

The main door to the mortuary swings open and Nik's father sweeps into the room.

Everyone stops what they're doing to stare at

him, unsure how to cope with the fact that the High Priest is entering the lowest level of the mummification suites. Normally, he spends most of his day in his office dealing with the administrative side of running the temple.

"You're all dismissed for the day," he says loudly. "Except for apprentices Nikare and Ankhesenamun. I need their assistance." He gestures for the two of us to go join him.

Either people will think Nik is being punished by his father and has dragged me along with him, or they'll assume we're getting a job because of who Nik is. I don't mind which, they'll both result in very few questions.

The others left in the room say their goodnights and make their way out, leaving the three of us alone.

Nerves flutter in my stomach no matter how much I try to get them under control. I don't think it helps that we have absolutely no idea whether or not there are going to be more bodies missing when we check the mummy storage room.

"All right, come with me," High Priest Ahmose instructs, heading in the direction of the dry room.

This one is bigger than the one in which they stored the bodies for our mummification test, and includes several bodies already placed in their coffins. There's an eerie sense of calm throughout the room, like the dead know they're waiting to journey on to the next life.

"Check the bodies and tell me if there are any you think are missing," he instructs, heading towards the line on the left.

"Which end do you want to start at?" Nik asks me.

"I'll take this one, if you go to the other end?"

He nods and heads away from me. I miss his presence almost instantly, but I ignore it and head towards the body closest to me. I reach out to touch the person's arm, but stop before I do.

I have a better way of checking the bodies that doesn't feel as bad as squeezing their arm.

I reach out and place my hand on the body's forehead and focus my senses. Almost instantly I can sense the embalmed body within, though I don't linger long enough to discover anything more than the fact there's someone in there.

I move on to the next one, going swiftly down the bodies.

It isn't until I'm about two-thirds down the line that I find one with the body missing. "This one," I say loudly.

Both Nik and his father look over in my direction.

"How are you checking them so fast?" Nik asks, his expression somewhere between jealous and impressed.

"Khafre taught me a Blessed trick," I admit. "It's taken me a while to manage it without Matia by my side, but I can do it now. It'll let me check whether or not there's a body quickly."

"Handy," he says.

"If you don't mind, I'm going to check it myself," High Priest Ahmose says. He reaches out and takes the fake body's arm, pressing firmly. He nods. "I'm going to order this one to be x-rayed tomorrow. That will confirm what we're already sure of and give us a paper trail we may need. The word of two junior apprentices isn't going to go very far."

"We understand," Nik says.

"You said you've found four missing bodies over the past month?" he asks us.

Nik nods his head while I stay silent. Technically, I haven't found anything, and I've only actually seen one of them. But I trust Nik implicitly. If he says there have been three more, then I believe him.

"That makes it seem unlikely that there's only one body missing in this room. I have to assume the culprits will be stealing more bodies in the next week or so," the High Priest muses.

He has a point, but I don't know what any of us can do about it.

"I'm going to make it known that the two of you have received cleaning duty as punishment for some discretion."

"What?" Nik blurts. "But..."

The High Priest raises his hand to stop any further complaint. "I'm aware that you've not done anything wrong this time, Nikare."

"Then why are we being punished?" he asks.

"Because I don't want anyone else to know about this, which means the two of you need to spend your evenings here for the next few days to make sure nothing happens."

"Oh." Nik seems surprised.

"You want us to keep an eye out for the thief?" I ask.

"Precisely. But you are not to engage with them. If you see anything, you are to send a message straight to me. If I find out you've put yourselves in danger again, I'll have no choice but to make your punishment real." He looks between us with a stern expression on his face.

I appreciate that he doesn't want us to do anything stupid, but I don't see how it's going to be possible to stay out of danger's way if we're keeping an eye on things here.

"What are we supposed to do with that time?" Nik asks.

His father shrugs. "Anything you want. I'm sure you'll find some way to amuse yourselves."

"Why us?" I ask. "Why not ask someone with more authority in the temple?"

"Because no one is going to be suspicious of two junior apprentices. Even the two of you. They won't think twice about seeing you here, and if they do, they'll just wait until you leave," the High Priest says. "But that's why you're not to engage with them under any circumstances."

"Got it," Nik says.

"Good. Then you're dismissed for the evening. I'll tell your supervisor about your punishment in the morning." He turns to leave without saying another word, leaving the two of us on our own.

"I guess that's good?" I say to Nik.

He shrugs. "I suppose so."

"Do you think I can bring Matia with me?" I

don't like the idea of her being alone for so long, especially if this is going to last for a while.

"I assume so. We can bring a Senet board if you want to?"

"You just want a rematch because I beat you."

"Partly," he admits with a grin.

"At least we get to do it together," I say. "That's better than having to do it alone."

"The feeling is mutual. We'll have a great time and catch the thief."

"Technically, we'll be just telling your father so he can catch him," I point out.

"True, but it still counts."

"If you say so."

Chapter 16

I pick up my pawn and move it a few squares along the Senet board, getting it closer to the end and to victory.

"That was a lucky throw," Nik says as he picks up his glass of juice and takes a sip.

"There's no such thing as luck. I'm just that good at the game."

He chuckles. "Of course you are." He picks up the sticks and tosses them to find out how many squares he gets to move. He groans as he realises he's not going to beat me. "Why do you keep winning?"

"I told you, skill." I pluck one of the grapes from the bunch and pop it into my mouth. "Have I told you how grateful I am that you thought to bring food tonight?"

"Only a few times, I could always deal with more expressions of gratitude."

I chuckle.

Matia perks her head up at the sound and looks around with a sleepy expression on her face as she tries to work out what's going on.

I reach out and scratch her head to assure her everything is fine. Now she's gotten used to the mortuary this late at night, she doesn't seem particularly interested in exploring.

Which is probably true for me and Nik too. It's been a week without any incidents, and we've gotten used to it to the point that we have a blanket to sit on as well as our entertainment and food. It's almost cosy.

If I ignore how close we are to dozens of dead bodies.

A crash sounds from the other room, making both of us freeze.

"Is that someone?" I whisper.

"No idea," Nik responds. "I'll go check. You pack this up just in case."

"Got it." I clear the Senet board quickly, placing the pawns and throwing sticks under the surface of the board, and slip it back into my bag. The food follows quickly. "Matia, I need you to move," I whisper to my jackal.

She hops to her feet and off the blanket. I grab it and scrunch it up, not bothering to fold it.

Nik returns a moment later. "Someone's definitely there. We need to get out of the room so we can see if they're coming here."

I nod. "We can leave via the other door."

The three of us follow the alternative path around the mortuary until we're back in the main room with a view of the door to the dry storage room.

Three men with their heads covered enter the room we've just vacated, leaving no doubt that they're up to no good.

"Message your father," I whisper.

"Already on it." Nik pulls out his phone and sends off a quick message. "Should we hang around, or..."

I shake my head. "We're not supposed to put ourselves in harm's way, remember?"

"And we're going to stick to that?"

"You know we are." I grab his hand and tug him towards the exit.

To my surprise, he doesn't even try and fight me and goes along as I drag him outside.

Matia trots along beside us, clearly having no idea that we're doing anything serious. I suppose that's the disadvantage to bringing her with me.

I don't breathe easily until we're outside the front door, though it doesn't appear that the High Priest is here yet.

"What should we do now?" I ask.

"I don't know, I've never been in this situation before," he admits. "We should wait. If they leave, we might be able to see who they are."

I nod, that makes a lot of sense.

"Hey, what's a jackal doing around here?" one of the men calls from inside.

My eyes widen and I look around to try and find Matia, only to discover she's missing.

"What do we do?" Panic comes through my question, but there's nothing I can do to stop it. If we get caught, then I don't know what's going to happen, but it won't be good.

"You should kiss me," Nik whispers.

"What? No."

"Seriously, Ani."

"This isn't the time," I whisper back. Wait, what is the time?

"Kiss me so we don't get caught. They'll just think that we're out here because we want some privacy or something," he responds. "Hurry."

"Oh." Disappointment floods through me.

Disappointment? That's not the emotion I expect when it comes to kissing Nik.

I push the thought to the side. I'll deal with it later when I have the time. Right now, we need to avoid getting caught by body snatchers.

I go up on my toes and press my lips against Nik's, trying not to think about it too much.

He cups my cheek in his hand and snakes his other around my waist, pulling me closer to him as he kisses me back.

My mind clears of everything other than our kiss. It's more intense than I expect from something that's supposed to be to keep our cover intact.

Something about this feels right. Like it's been building and it was going to happen no matter what we did.

But that makes no sense. I don't like Nik that way. We're friends and nothing more. He said it himself that I was his best friend. No one kisses their best friend.

The footsteps of several people approaching

cuts through my haze and I pull back, ending our kiss, but not chasing away the lingering effects.

"I think they're about to leave," I whisper.

Nik nods. "We should stay close in case they look in our direction."

I want to ask him if that's just an excuse so he can kiss me again, but I don't. Something has changed between us, and I can't put my finger on precisely what it is.

Shouts sound from the direction of the living quarters, announcing the arrival of the High Priest and the guards he's brought with him.

I pull away from Nik, putting some much-needed distance between us. I'm not prepared for how cold it feels to be out of his arms.

I shake my head. I can't let myself get distracted by these kinds of thoughts. Not only will it cause problems for the job we're supposed to be doing, but it could ruin our friendship and I'm not okay with that.

"Matia, here," I call softly.

The jackal bounces up to me and presses her head against my leg.

"Stay," I instruct her.

Shouts sound from inside the entrance to the

mortuary as High Priest Ahmose takes the body snatchers into custody.

They're dragged out of the building kicking and screaming.

"Fetch Hori," the High Priest instructs one of his guards. "Tell him to organise a search and priests to put the bodies back into the right place. He should keep the number of people involved to a minimum, I don't want this getting out to the general populace."

Nik and I make our way over to him, receiving a nod of his head in acknowledgement.

"Thank you for your help," he says to us both.

"You're not going to tell us what happened?" Nik asks, clearly hurt by the lack of information.

"I'll tell you in a debriefing after the festival," the High Priest responds. "Right now, I expect you to head to bed and not to say a word to anyone who isn't already aware of the situation."

"Got it," Nik mutters.

"You're dismissed."

With nothing else for it, the two of us start heading towards the living quarters with Matia running around us in circles.

The silence between us is deafening, but I have no idea how to change that.

What am I supposed to say?

The kiss is confusing to say the least. It felt like it was more than just a way to stop us getting caught, but there's no reason for that. We're nothing more than friends. Besides, there's a good chance it was just the adrenaline of the moment that made it feel like that, and in the morning, we'll both have forgotten it.

Which is just what I'm going to do. I'll sleep on it and decide what I have to say then. It's not like we're going to ruin our friendship in the course of an evening.

"Good night," I murmur once we reach the door of the living quarters and have to part ways. It's probably a good thing that he has to go back to his father's house.

"Night, Ani, sleep well," Nik responds, and if I'm not mistaken, there's something off in his voice too.

It's a strange turn of events to the end of our evening, especially when we didn't really do anything to catch the body snatchers other than being lookouts, but that was what the High Priest needed from us, so that's what we did. Sometimes, life is about listening to your superiors.

I pause before entering the building, trying to

think of what to say to Nik, but I can't think of anything. I push thoughts out of my mind and head inside. I climb the stairs to my room, wishing I had the energy for a bath but that will have to wait for the morning.

The moment I unlock the door to my room, Matia runs in and hops onto the bed, curling up in her normal spot and looking like she's been asleep for hours.

I switch my clothes for a nightshirt and slip in beside her. I should do other things before sleeping, but all I can do is fixate on the events of the evening. I press my fingers to my lips, still feeling the echo of my kiss with Nik.

One thing that's becoming clear is that I desperately need to see Neffie in person. At least the Tamesas festival starts tomorrow and we plan on going in a couple of days. I can talk to her then.

Chapter 17

The atmosphere created by the festival-goers is even more infectious than it has been in previous years. I'm not sure what's making this Tamesas festival better than the others, but there's something in the air that makes it feel that way.

And it's only day three. Things normally build until the final day when a huge celebration takes place and the barges of all of the gods and goddesses take to the river Thames and make the journey to Tamesas' temple. It's always been a spectacle, and that was before I held any particular affinity for one of the gods.

"You seem distracted," Neffie says, drawing my attention back to her. "You've ignored every stall selling sweet cakes, that's not like you."

I sigh. "There's lots going on at the temple." Stalls pass on either side of us as we make our way through the festival grounds, but we don't stop at any of them.

"And with your love life," she prompts.

I give a sharp laugh. "There hasn't been much time for that, I've been on cleaning duty for the past week." Though I suppose my kiss with Nik would count as a love life problem.

As would the fact that the two of us have been avoiding one another since.

And I hate it. I feel like I've lost something precious and I want it back.

"How is life at Bastet's temple treating you?" I ask. "Are you still having that fling with one of Ptah's apprentices?"

She wrinkles her nose. "No, I am not. It turned out he had girls at every temple in London."

"Ouch."

"It's fine, I wasn't that into him," she admits. "I'm not in a rush to find love. Not all of us have a prince fawning after us."

I sigh. "Right, a prince." The flicker of lanterns at one of the stalls catches the corner of my eye and draws my attention briefly to it.

"Shouldn't you be more excited about that?" she

asks. "You said he's been sending you presents." She looks me up and down as if she's expecting me to be wearing one right now.

"He does send gifts, yes. And they're always beautiful."

"But?"

"I'm just not sure whether he's right for me."

"Oh?"

I open my mouth to answer, but stop as I find myself standing in front of the last person I'm ready to talk to.

"Hey, Nik." I give an awkward half-wave which he returns in kind.

"Are you having a good time?" he asks, barely looking at Neffie.

"Mmhmm. You?" Eurgh, why do I sound so weird?

"Yes, good thanks."

"We're going to get something to eat," I say, trying to avoid eye contact.

"Ah, right, enjoy yourselves."

"We will. I'll see you back at the temple?"

He nods and waves goodbye, leaving me with Neffie and more confused than ever.

I resist the urge to turn and watch Nik leave. She slips her arm through mine and flashes me an expression that I know means we're going to have to have a talk about what just happened.

"We kissed," I blurt before she can ask me anything.

"You and Ramesses? It's about time. You've been dating for a few months," she says. "Though I don't know why that would make things between you and Nik weird."

"No, I kissed Nik," I correct her. "Ramesses tried to kiss me and I pushed him away."

"Oooooh. Well that makes more sense."

"It does?"

"Well, yes. I'm pretty sure he's half in love with you."

"Ramesses?" He doesn't seem that way.

"Nik."

"No, he's not, we're friends."

"Well, you think you are. And I'm pretty sure Nik thinks you are too, but anyone with eyes can see there's more between you," she says as if it's a matter of fact.

"What? No. There isn't. I don't like Nik that way."

"In which case tell me why you've kissed Nik but pushed Ramesses away?" Neffie asks.

I let out a small groan. "It's not like that. I kissed

Nik because otherwise, we were going to get caught if we didn't."

"Mmhmm."

"It meant nothing."

"If you say so." Neffie's face says she's completely convinced. "And how was it?"

I consider the best way to answer without making it seem like I'm completely into Nik, but I don't think there is one.

"It's the best kiss I've ever had," I admit. "But now he's avoiding me..."

"And let's guess, you're avoiding him too?"

"I mean, I suppose I am, yes."

"That's a classic Ani move. Don't you remember when you had that huge crush on Djoser and you refused to even be in the same room as him?"

"I don't have a crush on Nik."

The salty smell of frying potato reaches my nose and I steer Neffie in the direction of it.

"Oh no, you're much further gone than a crush." Her face says it all.

I groan. "But that just complicates things. Nik's my friend, I don't want to ruin that."

"Tell me how avoiding one another isn't going to do that?"

"I hate it when you're right," I mutter.

"I know you do, but it doesn't change the fact I am."

"So what do I do?"

"That depends. I think the main thing is that you have to talk to him. And I don't mean like whatever that was." She waves back in the direction we've come from. "You have to actually talk to him. Then you'll either work past it so you're both friends, or you'll turn into something more."

"I suppose Matia does approve of him, that's a definite pro."

Neffie lets out a small laugh. "And what does she think of Ramesses?"

"They've never met."

She raises an eyebrow.

I sigh. "Ramesses keeps inviting me to go with him to formal events, and while they're interesting, it's making it hard to properly get to know him."

"Ah, I can understand that."

"But I don't know how to ask him to change it, especially after I pushed him away when he tried to kiss me. I'm not sure there's any coming back from that."

"If he likes you, there will be," Neffie assures me. "But it sounds like you might not mind too much if you never hear from him again."

I bite my bottom lip. Is she right? I've always been annoyed by Ramesses' timing, but I don't think that means I don't want to spend time with him. At the same time, he's a prince, and I've never really felt like I can say no to attending events with him.

"Why is this so complicated?" My question comes out whinier than I intend it to, but luckily for me, my best friend just laughs.

"Because we're no longer ten."

"Then I want to be ten again."

"Turning back time isn't something we can do," she points out.

"I know."

"But what we can do is not talk about boys or temples for the rest of the day. We can just get ourselves lots of food and play some of the games and focus on having a good time."

"I like the sound of that. I've missed you."

"Right back at you," Neffie responds. "It's the one thing I dislike about being at Bastet's Temple."

"Does that count as temple talk?" I ask.

"Oh, you're right, it's time to ban it."

I let out a light laugh, relieved to be around my best friend again. I'm going to make the most of the time I can spend with her at the festival, especially as we both have the money from our apprentice-ships to spend. It may not be a huge amount, but we don't have to pay for food or accommodation, so it adds up quickly, especially if we plan on staying at the temple for a long time.

Which means that today is for enjoying myself. I'm not going to think about Nik, or Ramesses, or the dead.

Today is going to be about me and my lifelong best friend.

Chapter 18

A knock sounds on my bedroom door, causing me to frown. I have no idea who is going to be on the other side at this time.

"Come in," I call.

The door swings open and Nik steps inside.

Even I know I look surprised. Though I have to admit that he doesn't look any more comfortable than I do.

He stands in the doorway wringing his hands together and looking like he has about three thousand things to say without knowing how to put any of them into words.

Matia doesn't seem to be as nervous as we are and bounces over to him for scratches.

Nik smiles at the jackal and reaches out to tickle the top of her head. "Hello."

"Hey."

"Can I come in?" he asks.

"Aren't you already inside?"

He glances down at the ground. "I suppose so. But you didn't know it was me and things are weird between us right now."

I raise an eyebrow. "You noticed?"

"It's hard not to."

I let out a loud sigh. "Come in and close the door." I gesture to the chair by my dressing table. I'd normally invite him to sit on the bed, but somehow that feels too intimate for the way things are between us.

As soon as he's sat down, I do the same.

"Can we not be weird about this?" I blurt.

Nik raises an eyebrow.

"It's just that we're friends and I don't want to ruin that," I admit. "So can we just stop being weird and avoiding each other?"

He nods. "I'd like that."

"Good. I'm glad that's out of the way."

Matia seems to decide we're not doing anything interesting and hops up onto the bed and lies down with her head on my knee.

I stroke her head absentmindedly.

"So what made you actually decide to visit today?" I ask, assuming that he didn't come just to talk about the weirdness between us.

"Father talked to me about the body-snatching thing."

"Oh?" Pain lances through me as I realise I've been left out of the conversation.

"It was just over dinner. I asked him if he was going to do a debriefing with us."

"I take it the answer was no?"

"It was."

"Professional," I mutter.

"He claims it's because the matter is already solved and it's nothing for us to worry about."

I frown. "That doesn't make any sense."

"I don't think so either," Nik admits.

"So what are we missing?"

"I'm not sure. Father didn't like the way the organ thefts reflected on the temple, maybe it's something to do with that?"

"Two scandals back-to-back wouldn't look good to anyone. Is there a chance he could lose his job as High Priest if it got out?"

"Potentially, but I'm not sure how that kind of thing works."

"Maybe we should find out? I could ask Khafre how it works next time I have a Blessed lesson?"

"Do you think you can trust him?"

"Honestly? I don't know." The only person I trust completely is the one sitting opposite me, but I don't say that. We may agree that we want to put a stop to the weirdness between us, but there's still some of it there. "I have no reason not to trust him. He is the one that taught me how to be able to tell whether or not a body is actually there."

"I suppose the question is whether the timing of that was coincidental, or if he was trying to tell you something."

I frown. "Are you trying to suggest that his lessons were designed to help me work out what was going on?"

"It's a possibility. What does your gut say?"

"Huh. That's what Khafre said to me at the end of our last lesson."

"He asked you what your gut said?" Nik seems more confused than anything else.

"No, he told me to trust my gut because that was the way Anubis would make his will known to me."

"Cryptic."

"A little."

"So what is Anubis saying?"

"Are you really trying to call my gut feelings Anubis?"

He shrugs. "If that's what works. So, what does it say?"

"That I think it was just a coincidence that I learned how to sense the dead within their wrappings, but that there's definitely more to it than we've been told."

"And than my father wants to admit."

"Exactly."

"So I'm guessing the ban on getting into trouble is going to be lifted?" he asks, a familiar twinkle in his eye.

I'm relieved to see it.

"Yes, I'll lift the ban on getting into trouble. I'll need to if we're going to investigate this."

"I'm glad you've finally seen the light."

I laugh, taking us both by surprise.

Nik smiles at me, and I know in that moment that everything is going to be all right between us. I don't think we're going to be able to avoid talking about the kiss and how it felt for long, but if we manage to get our friendship back on track, then I don't think that's going to matter. When the subject comes up in the future, we'll be able to talk it through and come to some kind of conclusion.

Whatever that may be.

I don't dwell on how different that feels from when I think about what happened with Ramesses. It's clear our relationship isn't the same.

I push the thoughts out of my head and focus on the present.

"I'm sorry I've been avoiding you," I blurt.

"Same," Nik responds. "And I'm sorry I asked you to kiss me, I didn't think it through and it was just the first thing that came into my head."

"It's okay. So long as we can be friends again."

"We'll always be friends."

But we could also be more.

The expression on his face suggests I'm not the only one to be having that thought.

Now the air is cleared between us, we can focus on what really matters.

Discovering what's going on with the missing bodies, and why Nik's father doesn't want to do anything about it.

Thank you for reading *Initiate of the Jackal,* I hope

you enjoyed it. Ani's series concludes with *Novice Of The Afterlife:* https://books.authorlauragreenwood. co.uk/noviceoftheafterlife

If you want to learn how to play Senet (the game Ani and Nik were playing) you can download a printable board and instructions for free here: https://books.authorlauragreenwood.co.uk/ 1vb66km9ru

Author Note

Thank you for reading *Initiate Of The Jackal*, I hope you enjoyed Ani's second book.

Diving back into Ani's world was so much fun, especially as I got to explore her budding friendship with Nik more. I'll admit that their relationship has progressed in a completely different way than I originally planned, but that's part of what makes it so much fun!

It may not surprise you to know that Tamesas (the god of the Thames) wasn't a god worshipped by the Ancient Egyptians as the historical empire didn't expand as far as the UK. The name of the god comes from the Brittonic name for the river.

If you're interested in learning more about

Senet, it is a chess-adjacent style board game and you can find out more about it on my website!

If you want to keep up to date with new releases and other news, you can join my Facebook Reader Group or mailing list.

Stay safe & happy reading!

- Laura

Get A Free Apprentice Of Anubis Story

Is learning the art of mummification everything Dhara wants it to be?

After Dhara is chosen as one of the newest apprentices at the London Temple of Anubis, she's thrown into life at the temples, from learning about embalming, to the protective amulets used for the dead.

With the help of her mentor, she learns precisely what she needs in order to make it to ordination and to become a full Priestess Of Anubis.

-

Duty To The Dead is a standalone companion story to The Apprentice Of Anubis series, an urban fantasy set in an alternative version of London where the Egyptian Empire never fell. Duty To The Dead can be read as a standalone. The events take place during the events of Death Of The Pharaoh through to Court Of The Queen.

You can download Duty To The Dead for free here: https://books.authorlauragreenwood.co.uk/dhara

Also by Laura Greenwood

You can find out more about each of my series on my website.

- Obscure Academy: a paranormal romance series set at a university-age academy for mixed supernaturals. Each book follows a different couple.
- The Apprentice Of Anubis: an urban fantasy series set in an alternative world where the Ancient Egyptian Empire never fell. It follows a new apprentice to the temple of Anubis as she learns about her new role.
- Forgotten Gods: a paranormal adventure romance series inspired by Egyptian mythology. Each book follows a different Ancient Egyptian goddess.
- Amethyst's Wand Shop Mysteries (with Arizona Tape): an urban fantasy murder mystery series following a witch who teams up with a detective to solve murders. Each book includes a different murder.
- Grimm Academy: a fantasy fairy tale academy series. Each book follows a different fairy tale heroine.

- Jinx Paranormal Dating Agency: a paranormal romance series based on worldwide mythology where paranormals and deities take part in events organised by the Jinx Dating Agency. Each book follows a different couple.
- Purple Oasis (with Arizona Tape): a paranormal romance series based at a sanctuary set up after the apocalypse. Each book follows a different couple.
- Speed Dating With The Denizens Of The Underworld (shared world): a paranormal romance shared world based on mythology from around the world. Each book follows a different couple.
- Blackthorn Academy For Supernaturals (shared world): a paranormal monster romance shared world based at Blackthorn Academy. Each book follows a different couple.

You can find a complete list of all my books on my website:

https://books.authorlauragreenwood.co.uk/book-list

Signed Paperback & Merchandise:

You can find signed paperbacks, hardcovers, and merchandise based on my series (including stickers, magnets, face masks, and more!) via my website:

https://books.authorlauragreenwood.co.uk/shop

About Laura Greenwood

Laura is a USA Today Bestselling Author of paranormal romance, urban fantasy, and fantasy romance. When she's not writing, she drinks a lot of tea, tries to resist French macarons, and works towards a diploma in Egyptology. She lives in the UK, where most of her books are set. Laura specialises in quick reads, with healthy relationships and consent-positive moments regardless of if she's writing light-hearted romance, mythology-heavy urban fantasy, or anything in between.

Follow Laura Greenwood

- Website: www.authorlaura-greenwood.co.uk
- Mailing List: https://books.authorlauragreenwood.co.uk/newsletter
- Facebook Group: http://facebook.com/groups/theparanormalcouncil
- Facebook Page: http://facebook.com/authorlauragreenwood

- Bookbub: https://www.bookbub.com/
authors/laura-greenwood